Code Red Iran

Code Red Iran

Sydney Chaskalson

Cipher Press : Cambridge

2008

First published in 2008
by Cipher Press
41 St. Andrews Rd.,
Cambridge CB4 1DH,
UK

© Sydney Chaskalson 2008

ISBN 978-0-9559874-0-3

Front Cover image Annie Chaskalson
Back cover author photo Motti Direktor

Introduction

This book is a work of fiction, based on fact, and interspersed with autobiographical details. Most of what is written here exists. Iran and Ahmidjenehad of Iran exist, as do his continual threats to wipe Israel off the face of the earth. The Iranian atomic programme (at the time of writing) exists. Iran's uranium enrichment plants at Natanz, Bushweir and other sites exist, as do the Mojahedin-e-Khalk. Their attacks on the current Iranian theocracy are real, and the results of their attacks on the Iranian Revolutionary Guards are factual.

The Israeli commentators on Iran and its nuclear ambitions, quoted in this book, are real people. Their comments are culled from quotations in current Israeli newspapers. The characters in the book are fictional.

Although it is a work of fiction, everything related here exists as a possibility.

My heartfelt thanks are due to many people, without whose help this book could never have been written. My late wife, Edele, read and encouraged me in writing the earlier chapters. Four years later my present wife, Maureen, has been a daily source of encouragement, reading, re-reading, and commenting on each chapter. My sister-in-law, Lorraine Chaskalson, read the earlier chapters, and her comments, "Syd, go for it," were always at the back of my mind. My three children Harry, Michael and Marguerite, read and encouraged me to complete this book. Without the logistical help they presented at my birthday party in Prague, there is no way this book could have seen the light of day. Michael, an author in a very different sphere, organized the transition from manuscript to publication. My daughter-in-law,

Annie, created the cover and encouraged me at all times. My son-in-law, Motti Direktor, made a great author's photo.

Mr. D.J. Herda, Chairman of the American Society of Authors, read a synopsis of the early work and put me in touch with Lou Aronica, who critiqued the first two chapters and gave me some valuable insights on authoring a work of fiction. Zara Jackson edited most of the book and passed on lessons in creative writing.

Tamlyn Monson edited the final manuscript in great depth, from start to finish. She has done more than I had hoped for or expected in her editing work. Tamlyn, thanks a million.

In 2007 I was fortunate to be invited to the Annual Meeting of the American Jewish Committee in Washington. There I met and had the pleasure of discussing the Iranian situation with various high-ranking officers of the Israeli Defence Force. I will not mention their names, but thanks, *chaverim*, for your time and input, and thanks too for giving me an opportunity to speak Hebrew again.

This book is dedicated to the countless unsung heroes of the Mossad, who have kept Israel safe, often at the cost of their own lives.

Chapter 1

Netanya, Winter 2007

Even the new high-rise buildings, perched near the verge of the crumbling cliff face, could not stop the sheets of rain, driven in from the sea by the force of the west wind, from battering my old house. Shutters I had been meaning to repair over months of procrastination creaked ominously, threatening to blow away at any moment.

The twilight sky was darkening quickly, forecasting worse to come, and reminding me that the roof, too, was sadly in need of tender loving care, or – at the very least – new tiles. Against the howling voice of nature, punctuated as it was by the pitiful moans of the house, I barely heard the hammering at the door.

Rousing myself from the couch, I made my way to the hallway and peered through the peephole. Outside was my good friend Shimon, soaked to the skin, with what was left of his hair plastered to his forehead.

Propelled by the sheer force of the gale, he almost fell into the hallway as I opened the door. Well built at about 1.8 metres, Shimon was dressed for winter in a rain-resistant padded khaki jacket over a heavy, brown-checked flannel shirt. Brown in colour, the worn jump-boots sticking out from under his heavy corduroy slacks gave away his military background. Like me, he had been a paratrooper. We red berets were the only arm of the Israeli defence force to deviate from the standard-issue black boots.

A very fit forty – looking far younger – Shimon stood gasping for breath, his ruddy face dripping. The rain had defied his winter gear: water poured from every stitch of clothing, soaking wetly into my worn-out carpet. "What the hell brings you out at a time like this?" I demanded, incredulous. "Hell's business!" he gasped, looking down helplessly at his dripping clothes.

"Well, off with your jacket and boots," I urged. "Have a drink. Relax – tell me more."

He was having none of it. "No drink. No time," he panted, "come with me – you must see for yourself!"

There was no way I was going out there – he may have lost his mind, but I hadn't. "In this weather? You must be joking," I replied. "It's not the end of the world, let's sit down and wait the weather out. You can tell me all about it in the meantime."

But he was adamant. "The end of the world is just what it might be! We have to go now. Together, we might just be able to do something before it's too late!"

I'd known Shimon through three wars and five divorces – three of his; two of my own – but never before had I seen him so distraught. Impelled by his urgency, and much against my better judgment, I reluctantly pulled on my quilted goose-down *dubon*,* covered my head with its hood, and followed him into the night.

The driving rain had turned the road into an ankle-deep torrent of muddy brown water and, as the water soaked through my Nikes, making every step an effort, I cursed Shimon – and myself for humouring him.

Then, with a sudden, single flash of white, the storm blacked out every light in the city – a not-unusual winter occurrence, but a particularly inconvenient one under the circumstances. Now, only flashes of sheet lightning lit my path as I followed Shimon along the slippery, crumbling path that led down from the hotel-lined cliffs to the beach. Grasping at rain-soaked bushes to steady myself, tripping over roots and stones, I finally found myself standing next to Shimon near a dilapidated lifeguard tower that, in the gloom, appeared unlikely to see another summer.

Shimon's body, lighter and lither than mine, was tensely poised; his bearing reminiscent of our army days. His usually grinning, rounded face was frozen in an anxious mask,

---

* *Hebrew: Anorak, usually khaki in colour.*

heightening the deep shrapnel scar on his left cheek.

Suddenly, I saw the focus of his gaze. Tied to one of the uprights of the Lifeguard tower was not a sodden old sack, as I had first thought, but the bloody, lifeless body of what had once been a man.

My first thought was to call the police – why on earth had Shimon come to me in the first place? But as I moved closer, I finally understood the cause of his out-of-character panic. The face was familiar: Gidon Bar-Ziv, a man both Shimon and I had once known very well indeed.

Gidon was not only a close associate, but also a good friend. Twenty years ago, he had been our commanding officer back in Lebanon – where thunder of a different kind had reigned over our nights. Now he was head of a little-known counter-terrorist unit allied to Shin Bet, Israel's homeland security force. A secret unit, with a single aim: to root out suicide bombers carrying tactical nuclear weapons.

Shimon and I shared more history than just our failed marriages and careers in the red berets – now that we were past our prime, we had both been recruited by Gidon in an advisory capacity, to help train his new recruits in undercover skills and unarmed combat.

For a moment I was speechless. "How did you find him on a night like this?" I shouted into the rush of rain, after a long pause. Shimon looked at the waterlogged ground, searching for words. "He called me earlier; told me that an informer had some startling information. I was supposed to meet the two of them here," he began. "He wanted my opinion. Said he trusted my Arabic more than his to check out the guy's story." He caught the question in my eye. "I know. It must have been something really important – he usually worked alone, and his Arabic was really good."

Shimon's Arabic was fluent; he spoke it better than anyone I knew. But few in the unit struggled with the language. Gidon must have been onto some vital information, or maybe he'd had a hunch he was being deceived.

The two of us stood silent, water coursing down our necks as we stood rooted in the wet sand, the storm forgotten as an array of alarming possibilities opened up before us. Eventually, our eyes met once again. "Now what?" I said, continuing with the obvious: "We have to call the police."

Shifting from one leg to the other, Shimon sighed. "We're going to be pretty high on the suspect list," he said, looking apologetic. "No motive, but we both knew him well, and this is hardly the time and place for a friendly get-together."

"Thanks for that," I quipped, kicking myself for allowing him to talk me into this fool's errand. "Still, no option. We've got to call them. It won't be the first time we've had to talk ourselves out of a tight spot."

Shimon reached under his down jacket for his cellphone, dialed, and reported the bad news to the security officer on duty. "They'll contact the Shin Bet* liaison in Netanya," he told me, after pocketing the phone. "We must wait here and secure the scene until they arrive."

"In the meantime, we get even wetter – if that's possible!" I griped, looking longingly at the small patch of dryish sand sheltered by the lifeguards' platform. We couldn't go home, and the only shelter here was the crime scene, which had to be preserved. Feeling sorry for myself, I couldn't help reflecting how times had changed. Twenty years ago I was living on army rations in makeshift shelters, every luxury of home forgotten. Now it seemed I was a soft-bellied homebody. Nevertheless, we had a duty to carry out, with – but preferably without – the police. Gidon had been a close friend as well as our CO, and we had a better chance of solving his murder, and indeed avenging him, if we followed up the case ourselves – especially as it might directly concern our unit.

While we were waiting, Shimon and I discussed at great length the possibility that this might be a mafia crime. Netanya – a major coastal city on the route between Tel-Aviv and Haifa – has a population of well over 200,000 people, and is one of the most diversely populated towns in the cosmopolitan state of Israel. Like a small Miami, it is famed as much for its coastal splendour as for the headline-grabbing clashes of the competing mafias that continually vie for control of the city's criminal economy. Comprising immigrants from Libya, Morocco, Tunis and Algeria,

---

Israel's internal security service, also known as Shabak.

the criminal underground was originally controlled by north African Jews who arrived after Israel prevailed against seven Arab armies in the 1948 War of Independence. But they soon split into two competing bands, fighting for control of the burgeoning crime industry of gambling, sex, protection and drugs.

Yet there was even more to come for the once small, provincial tourist town, whose distinguishing features had previously been its thriving diamond-cutting industry, and the citrus-growing cooperative *moshavim** that skirted its edges, harking back a time when the city was no more than a tiny agricultural settlement of orange groves. Change came in the form of Russian immigrants who escaped the Soviet Union in the late seventies and mid-eighties. Some were Jews genuinely seeking a life in the Holy Land. Others, with shadier backgrounds, conjured up imaginary Jewish ancestry just to escape Russia's iron stranglehold. They revelled in their newfound freedom, establishing Russian mafias that pitted themselves against the established North African ones, bringing with them a new vice – international money laundering.

By the time the Shin Bet representative arrived, Shimon and I were in agreement that mafia involvement was unlikely. Gidon's contact had been a speaker of Arabic, and our comrade's conversation with Shimon had revealed nothing in the man's background that suggested a connection with our assortment of Hebrew-speaking mafias.

To our great relief, the Shabak liaison was someone we both knew: Meyer Jephet. Even before being recruited by the Shin Bet internal security service, Meyer had served briefly alongside us. Short and stocky, he had a tanned, lined face that seldom betrayed any emotion. Certainly he was more adept at obtaining information than giving it away. He made a formidable poker player, as our regular Thursday-night games attested.

Meyer, too, was dressed in waterproof winter gear, and, like us, was soon soaked to the skin as the gale pummeled the Netanya shoreline with sheets of rain and clouds of sea spray, erasing the city's famous beaches and coastal promenades in a grey haze.

* *Hebrew: settlements or villages.*

Waiting on the beach for the police to arrive, getting wetter and wetter, we told him all that we knew, and Meyer agreed with our reasoning: this was very likely a security-related crime.

By the time the Netanya Police finally made their entrance amid wailing sirens and flashing blue lights, the three of us were soaked to the skin. But their usual tardiness was a boon this time: without Meyer Jephet as an ally we would have spent the night in the Raziel Street jail. As it was, it took us nearly an hour to tell our story, and after faithfully promising to put it all down in writing, we were allowed to leave. We were to meet the investigating officer, Arik, at the Raziel Police Station at 10h00 the next day.

It was now past midnight. Shivering violently, we made our sad way back to my house, where we took turns in the shower and changed into dry clothes. The sight of my clothes hanging loosely off Shimon's fit frame filled me with a momentary nostalgia for my younger, leaner self, but it was soon forgotten as we nursed stiff cognacs and coffee on the couch, keen to feel our blood circulating again. There was so much to discuss, and, tired as we were, our conversation turned back to the night's horrible events. One thing was clear: Gidon's murder was not one for gain. Both the scene of the crime and the weather made this a certainty.

We asked ourselves the question we knew police would pose: "Who benefits?" No-one we knew had any grudge against Gidon – that ruled out all our friends and acquaintances, including the members of Gidon's unit. After the night's traumatic events, the sheer physical effort of climbing the cliffs, and the effects of the coffee and Cognac (which I always poured with a heavy hand), our brains were addled. We went round and round with half-finished ideas, and at long last decided that the best thing was to attempt a good night's sleep before our meeting with the police and Shin Bet. Once that was over, we could return and talk the whole matter over with clear heads.

I made up the long-unused spare bedroom for Shimon, and we wearily bid each other good night. It was not easy to surrender to sleep after all that had happened. My mind kept turning over and over, restlessly pondering the mystery before us. Eventually I remembered a box of sleeping pills prescribed years back – probably way past expired. After downing two, I closed the medicine cabinet and looked at my reflection for a moment. Dani

Mafouz, height 1.83 metres, overweight at 85 kg. Unlike Shimon, I still had all my hair, though I couldn't help noticing that the grey was now rapidly overtaking the black, stark against the olive complexion I had inherited from my Jewish-Iranian mother. Otherwise, I looked more and more like my father, recently deceased. German-born, he had fled to Iran as the holocaust began to unfold, changing his name to Mafouz to blend in with the Iranian Jewish community. Tired as I was now, I caught a glimpse of his aging face in my own.

I turned back to bed, hoping the sedatives would kick in soon. After a few minutes of tossing and turning, I finally fell into a dream-filled sleep.

Chapter 2

The next day dawned clear and bright. It was hard to believe that only a few hours ago we had been in a near hurricane. After an early breakfast, we wrote a brief report for the police and handed it in to Arik at the police station. It was difficult to believe that any major event could be reduced to so few words.

Now, Shimon was striding up and down the living room — he always said that he could only think on his feet. Once more, we discussed at length the possibility of a Mafia connection to Gidon's murder.

"There's no clear-cut connection," I reflected, "but we can't rule anything out. We must keep all possibilities open." There were only two possibilities, as far as I was concerned. Either Gidon had been murdered by the so-called informer, or there was a more complex case to investigate, in which the informer had also been either killed or kidnapped.

Shimon agreed. "If Gidon was murdered simply because he was Gidon, we can leave things in the hands of the police and Shin Bet. Only help out if they ask us. But if not, there's more to consider," he said. "First, Gidon might have been tortured — badly. Which means he might have been forced to reveal information about our unit."

"In which case," I interrupted, "they'll know about us. Especially you, as you were meant to meet him soon afterwards. We had better watch our backs."

Grinning, Shimon gave me a black look. "Your back is easy to watch," he quipped, "time you lost some weight. Now shut up and let me finish." He took a breath and continued. "Secondly, if the informer was genuine then it means that he had information for our unit."

"That means only one thing," I interjected. "The possibility of a terror attack with a tactical nuke." Shimon nodded. "And with our government's eye-for-an-eye policy, the whole Middle East could go up in flames. That kind of nuclear holocaust could spread world-wide," he said.

Stunned by this apocalyptic vision, I looked at him wide-eyed. "My God!" I exclaimed. "So that's what you meant last night when you said it might just be the end of the world! *Ya-allah**! We'd better act fast. If this informer was the real thing, we have to find him quickly, dead or alive. We're going to need a tracker," I went on. We both knew that meant our Bedouin friend Gadir.

Gadir preferred to be called by his Hebrew nickname, Gadi. Gadi was the word for a kid or young goat, and Gadir had certainly lived up to the name as a *gashas* in our para battalion – a combination scout and tracker. Small and slight in build, he was uncommonly agile, with a unique ability to pick up a trail from a few crushed leaves and some dusty impressions in the dirt.

Now 55 years old, Gadir was no longer on active service, but had lost none of his skills. Few, if any, of the younger Bedouin trackers could match his fantastic ability. These days, he lived in a small Bedouin encampment near Hadera, looking out on a small forest and an even smaller lake filled by the winter rain. To supplement his pension, he worked transporting fresh produce to and from the Netanya *shouk*.** Situated in the centre of the older part of the city, the *shouk* stretched for several city blocks, and its merchants sold everything from vegetables, clothing and household products to furniture and electronics. This was the obvious place to find him, and it was only 10 minutes away from my house. We drove there immediately.

Parking my jeep in the only free illegal parking place, we entered a world far removed from the modernistic Netanya beach front. Covering close on a square kilometre in the heart of the city, the *shouk* could have been the centre of any Middle Eastern city of

---

* *Originally from Arabic: My God.*
** *Hebrew: Open-air market.*

the past few centuries. Stall after stall displayed brightly coloured piles of fresh fruit and vegetables, far better in both quality and price than any found in the world's best supermarkets. Open-fronted butcher's shops stood cheek-and-jowl with vendors of fresh fish – offered live from crowded tanks. Piles of exotic herbs perfumed the atmosphere with the scents of cardamom, basil and oregano.

As we navigated the market, clothing, both new and second hand, was being pawed over by recent immigrants. It seemed that these newcomers from the former Soviet Union could hardly believe that such quantities of food and clothing were available, if not for the taking – which a few did anyway – then at least for the bargaining.

The sellers competed with each other by shouting out their produce and prices above the sound of customers bargaining loudly in a variety of Hebrew accents. The voices of newly arrived Russian immigrants, clutching their trademark plastic bags, sounded guttural against the ancestral Yemenite, Moroccan, Libyan and Iraqi accents of local Israelis. The voices were a reminder of how Netanya had swelled with the waves of immigration that followed its founding in 1928: first, the pioneers from eastern Europe, then waves of Jewish immigrants from Arab countries – Libya, Morocco, Algeria, Yemen and Iran – and a large colony of English-speaking visionaries from South Africa, England and America. In the early years, the communities had existed side by side, tending to move in contiguous social circles. But while the original immigrants had kept to each other's company, their different cultures were disappearing as their Hebrew-speaking children intermarried, merging into a single Israeli nation.

Our ears battered by the polyglot cacophony of vendors and buyers in this multi-coloured mass of people and products, Shimon and I hurried as fast as we could in search of Gadir. We came across him trying in his best broken English to give directions to some English-speaking residents who, by the looks of them, would much rather have been anywhere else, but were determined to buy in the *shouk* so they could boast of bargains to their supermarket-shopping friends. He looked much the same as when we had last seen him on our annual three-week tour of *miluim* reserve duty: 1.7 metres tall; brown and wrinkled as the pecan nuts sold nearby. His lean, still-lithe body was dressed summer and winter in old army fatigues, and today was no exception.

"Gadi!" Shimon shouted, "Come over here! We need your help."

Gadir smiled to see us. "What for? To carry your shopping?" he joked in Hebrew, poking fun at the perennial English speakers, "can you not see that I am busy with real ladies and gentlemen, who speak softly?"

"Gadi, we need the world's best tracker!" I yelled over the noise.

"Oh-oho! In that case I might just have some free time," he shouted back, freeing himself and hurrying towards us.

Driving back to the beach, we brought Gadir up to date on the events of the last few hours. He was visibly shaken and could hardly believe what had happened.

"Gidon was like family to me," he said, finally. "It was he who did the impossible and arranged for my family and me to live near Hadera. He visited often, and we would sit for hours drinking cardamom-flavoured Arabic coffee and talking about old battles – how they could have been refought."

After a long pause, Gadi continued: "It was amazing how fluent his Arabic was. We often spoke in Arabic. I loved hearing how his family escaped across Europe to avoid the holocaust, and about their many adventures on the way. And he would always insist on hearing Bedouin folklore…" Gadi's voice trailed off into a stricken silence. Several minutes later, he began again.

"We must avenge him," he declared. "It is my duty to help you find his killer." Gadir's code of honour made this a blood feud that could end only in death – that of the murderer, or his own.

Back at the beachfront, the three of us descended the steep slope until we arrived at the roped-off crime scene. The officer on duty had been warned to expect us, and as Shimon and I hovered close by, Gadir made his cautious way to the lifeguard tower where we had found Gidon's body the previous night.

"It's not going to be easy," he told us. "You have waited too long before calling me here! Look – there are all the footprints of the clumsy policemen, and here you can see the marks left by the stretcher-bearers who took away the body. Still, it is easy to separate the police-issue boots from the others," he reflected.

"Here I see your heavy steps, Dani," he continued, pointing out trail of deeper tracks, "and here are Shimon's. These are Gidon's," he said, pointing elsewhere, "I still remember them clearly from the old days. The prints tell us he was waiting for someone – you can see he was pacing across a small area. Luckily the tower's platform has preserved most of the prints."

Suddenly, Gadir stopped talking and bent even closer to the ground. "Look! See these marks – they are very faint, but you can see that they are different from all the others. There is a block-shaped pattern, with an oval toe print from a steel reinforcement. Only one source for those – Russian desert boots, the old type!"

He rubbed his chin. "Could be Syrian, Iraqi or Iranian. Shallow prints, so he is not too big a man. And they lead up behind Gidon's prints, so they were not face to face. It looks like he crept up on Gidon and struck him down before he knew what had happened."

"Then he must have been an expert tracker, like you," I said, remembering how Gadi had tracked a group of terrorists on their way back from a mission in Israel – coming up right behind them.

"Gidon was not easily surprised, and he would have been cautious. There's always the chance of a surprise attack with these covert meetings," Shimon agreed. "We're looking at a trained killer, not your everyday, spur-of-the-moment murderer, who acts first and thinks afterwards. This was obviously well planned and carried out."

"Well, now we know when, where, and how," I said, "and we most likely know why, as well. It must have been something to do with our unit, which is bad news. What we don't know is who he is, who he represents, and where we can find him."

Gadir was not so easily deterred, "We know the prints; all we have to do is trace them back." Bending forward, with his face near the ground, Gadir left the roped-off area and circled round and round. "Here! Now I have him – no other prints to confuse things. Damn this rain! It's washed out most of them, but you can still see traces on the rocky ground. He was not heading for the main road, as we might have expected. He exited through the bush towards the Surf Crest Hotel!"

Chapter 3

The Surf Crest Hotel had a dubious reputation. Far enough out of town for its car park to go unnoticed, yet close enough to be reached within 15 minutes, it naturally attracted couples looking for a discrete and speedy rendezvous. Late at night, the dance hall was said to become a secret casino, which the police never seemed to raid.

The owner-manager, Mario Hajaj, was related to half the Netanya underworld, and subscribed generously to all the right charities. We suspected that he also had Arab connections. It was an open secret that cars regularly disappeared from the Surf Crest lot at night and made their way over the border through Tulkarim into the West Bank. The victims were usually unsuspecting clients of Mario's ladies of the night – they had no recourse to the law without giving away their nefarious motives for visiting the hotel in the first place. Undoubtedly, the Surf Crest Hotel got an additional income stream from the Palestinian car-theft industry.

As Gadir had thought, the hotel was indeed the end of the trail that led from the beach. "OK," said Shimon, "now that we know where he went, we have to find out exactly who he is."

"I say we just storm in there, talk tough, and force the information out of Mario," I said. "He acts like a big shot, but the bottom line is he's just a would-be gangster. He may not know exactly what we're involved in, but he knows our Shin Bet connection. He'll cave if we're brutal enough."

Shimon shook his head. "No, Dani," he said thoughtfully. "That would mean giving away everything we know too early in the game. We need a more subtle approach."

Gadir agreed. He had an idea. "The way I am dressed," he said, in his ever-formal Hebrew, "I could be any Bedouin job seeker off the street. Mario is always looking for workers. He pays off the books – in cash, but way below the going wage. The youngsters in our community come here when they're desperate, but they never stay long. I am sure I can get a job, meet all the staff, and find out who's who – and just which one is our man."

I gave up on my gung-ho plan, and Shimon and I resolved to pose as restaurant customers, while Gadi approached the hotel from the back entrance, as befitting a job-seeker. That way, we'd be on hand if Gadi needed us, and we could catch up on our missed breakfast with coffee and baklava. We took seats in the lounge, carefully choosing a vantage point from which we could see the path leading to the back entrance.

Time passed – maybe too much time – and, under Shimon's disapproving eyes, I ordered more baklava. After all, it was now way past lunch time.

"You know, Shimon, maybe this wasn't such a good idea after all," I mused, concerned about the fate of our friend. "Maybe Gadi's got into some sort of trouble. Let's try it my way. I'd love to beat the shit out of Mario." It seemed as good a time as any to flex our muscles.

"*Savlanoot*,* Dani," he urged me in his ever-calm voice, "you always want to jump bull-headed into trouble. Softly-softly catch 'ee monkey, as the English say."

"Where does that softly-softly bit come from anyway," I asked, crestfallen.

"Don't really know, Dani," he said, looking toward the path Gadi had taken. "Maybe from the Brits – colonial India, or something like that. Worth remembering for you, though."

As I picked up my coffee cup again, knowing it was now too cold to drink, a side door opened and Mario entered. Standing only 1.75 metres tall, he wore his usual crocodile-skin lift-up shoes. His dark-skinned face and small, darting, red-rimmed brown eyes made him look like a giant rodent.

He was dressed in pressed jeans and a shiny black shirt, unbuttoned almost to the navel. His hairy chest displayed a heavy

---

* *Hebrew: Patience.*

gold chain which hung unflatteringly close to his protruding pot belly. Greasy black hair framed his half-shaved face. Silently I wondered how he managed to sport a five-o-clock shadow 24 hours a day, seven days a week. And despite all this, he still thought that he was God's gift to womankind.

"I know you two," he said gruffly, his eyes flickering nervously. "What are you doing here?"

I was ready to put him straight for this less-than-warm welcome, but Shimon's diplomacy beat me to it. "Just waiting, Mario," he said, using the man's first name, as is the convention in Israel. "Dani's girlfriend is bringing round a friend to meet me." He winked, trying to put Mario at ease.

It was a good cover – the two of us were well known for our many brief romances and short-lived commitments. For my part, I couldn't blame either of my wives for leaving me. I had married both of them for their good looks, and for the fun times we had together. But those times grew few and far between with my frequent, long stints of army duty. When home, my love of sports and beer-drinking sessions with my army buddies left little time for marital togetherness, and in both cases we slowly drifted apart, and eventually parted amicably. Nowadays, they and their new husbands were like an odd sort of extended family to me. Shimon, on the other hand, was like a brother, and we double-dated quite often – though on more than one occasion recently I had looked rather covetously upon his new flame, Adinah.

"*Hu!* Shimon, thought you'd know better than to trust this one," he said, giving me a disparaging look. "However! It just so happens that I can fix you up with two very nice ladies. Cost you a bit, but better than waiting for nothing!"

"Thanks, but no thanks, Mario," Shimon replied. "I only like the amateur league." As it happened, Adinah was the manageress of a sex shop in the city, but she was certainly not a working girl of that sort! Shimon looked at his watch – 15h30. "Still, seeing it's getting so late, maybe you could bring us two nice, cold Goldstar beers," he added.

"My pleasure. After you've had a few beers, you'll rethink my kind offer – you really won't regret it." So saying, Mario moved off, and soon reappeared with our beers.

Shimon remained unperturbed as the winter dusk began to fall at 17h30. "Well, Dani, better sitting here and drinking than waiting outside in the dark. Seems Mario is a real slave driver." He was convinced that if anything serious had happened to Gadi, we would have heard or seen something suspicious. I was less certain – anything could happen behind closed doors. "I'm just sorry we've been under Mario's nose all day," I muttered. His offers of professional services had been reiterated several times now, and I was beginning to feel we would have to accept just to back up our cover story. "At least the beer is cold," I remarked, frowning at my glass.

We sipped the beers slowly, trying to drag out the time, as the sky grew darker and darker outside. I looked at my watch: 18h00. Nearly five hours had passed since we had sat down in the faded velour lounge chairs. Surely some of the kitchen staff should be leaving by now, I thought, looking out toward the staff entrance. Just then, a trickle of poorly clothed workers began leaking from the building. I nudged Shimon, and as he turned his head, we spotted Gadir leaving with the others.

I called for Mario, but there was no sign of life behind the bar. Tossing a 100-shekel note on the table to pay our tab, we left hurriedly and discreetly followed the Arabic-speaking workers along the road to the bus stop. Only at the last moment did we get onto the same bus that Gadir boarded. We ignored each other, until the bus finally stopped at the Central Bus Station, in the centre of Netanya. Everyone got off, and Gadir walked east, towards the main highway.

We followed him at a distance, until he walked into the all-night Trupha pharmacy. Seeing our opportunity, we followed, picked up a couple of over-the-counter items, and, as we left, deliberately bumped into Gadir at the doorway.

"You clumsy idiots," he muttered, smiling, as the three of us moved into the street, "I saw you following me a kilometre away!"

Together, we walked into a *beit*-café* nearby. Once we were seated at a back-corner table, Gadir looked around and nodded.

---

* *Hebrew: A small coffee house.*

"Now we can speak," he said seriously.

"Thank God everything's OK," I said. "We were beginning to worry about you."

Gadi smiled. "I bet it was you Dani! Shimon has always been better at the waiting game."

Shimon met Gadi's eye with an affirmative look. "You know Dani; he thinks that worrying helps! But here we are, all together and surprisingly unharmed" – a jab at me again – "so, tell us your news."

Gadi nodded. "All in good time," he said, an eyebrow raised. "But the least you can do is order some refreshments – I am sure that the two of you did not starve while I was sweating throughout the day."

Just at that moment, the waitress came up to our table. "Tuna and egg sandwiches for three, on fresh rolls, mind, and three coffees – hot and strong!" I ordered. As soon as she left, Gadir spoke.

"I think I have the man. As soon as I asked for work, Mario said, 'You're in luck, one of my kitchen staff left without notice today.' The only conditions were that I started at once and knew how to chop vegetables for salad. Fifty shekels a day cash, six nine-hour days a week.

"The working day starts at 08h30 and ends at 17h30 and you're paid only for the hours you work. So I walked away with a half day's pay," he winked, patting his pocket. "When I got to the kitchen, it turned out the regular chopping knife had disappeared along with the man who had left. Mario made a big deal of the fact that anything lost on my watch would be deducted from my salary."

"Looks like you struck gold, Gadi," Shimon exclaimed. Looking at me meaningfully, he continued, "And no need to bust in and spill all our secrets."

"OK, OK. *Slicha,**" I apologised. "Gadi, you were great! Now, tell us what else you learned." At that moment, the waitress returned with our orders. Gadi attacked his sandwich hungrily, and as soon as the waitress was out of hearing, he continued speaking between mouthfuls.

* *Hebrew: Patience.*

"I got friendly with the other workers – said how lucky I was to get work so quickly. Not much money, but at least in cash, paid each day.

"The kitchen helpers were Musa, from Nablus, and his friend Achmed, who came from Tulkarim. Musa complained a lot about Mario – how he pays cash just to dodge tax and national insurance – but said he had no choice but to stay because there was no work back in Nablus. I asked if it was the work that drove their co-worker away, but they said he told them it was family business that had taken him away so suddenly.

"Achmed lived in Tulkarim, as I said, and hardly spoke to the man. But a friendly young man named Ebrahim, who was training to be a waiter, joined in our conversation; said the man's name was Jibril Tirawin. He apparently kept very much to himself – Ebrahim thought he must have been lonely here.

"He avoided speaking about himself for the most part, it seems. But one thing he let slip was that he had been away from his hometown in the West Bank for a long time, and that he was only killing time until he started his real job. Said that he was just earning pocket money here."

My eyes met Shimon's at this revelation. What kind of business could Jibril have expected to lift him out of minimum-wage slavery? Ebrahim had refused to say more about the job he had in mind. It was a family secret, he had said, and he could lose his position if he spoke about it.

Gadi went on, "At that point, Achmed chimed in; he'd seen Jibril at large political gatherings organised by Hamas. Achmed wasn't a member himself, but attended to hear what Hamas proposed to do to improve his life, and that of others like him. Achmed said he always stood outside the main crowd, but he saw Jibril right up front. Achmed was hoping Jibril would turn out to be one of the big shots in the organisation, *ins'halla** he might help all the workers improve their lives," Gadi looked sad at this. "It's hard to keep a family on what they earn."

"Did he say where Jibril lived?" I asked.

---

* *Arabic: God willing.*

"No, but I gathered it was not too far away. He chained up a bicycle outside the kitchen each day, so it must be fairly nearby."

"Gadi! You've done a fantastic job of work," said Shimon. "If it's nearby, and he was seen by Achmed at Hamas gatherings, it could only really be Tulkarim." His brow furrowed, "We have to get there somehow, and it's not easy. But Tulkarim, dangerous as it is, seems to be our next stop."

Chapter 4

I kicked off further discussion. "We have learnt two important things. One: Jibril was seen at Hamas meetings by a man who lives in Tulkarim. Two: he travelled by bicycle, which means that he was living not too far away. Tulkarim seems like our best bet. The question is, how do we get there without drawing attention to ourselves?" The town was a known Hamas stronghold, and to say that Israelis were unwelcome there was an understatement.

Shimon and Gadir shared my concern. "We can't travel on the main road; there's an army roadblock only two hundred metres from the main entrance to the town. If they let us through it'll be obvious that we have security clearance," said Shimon.

"There is a way to get there undetected," said Gadir. "I often deliver turkey meat to the *shouk* from the processing plant at Kibbutz Yad Chana. Only a fence separates the kibbutz from the north side of Tulkarim. It's already evening, so if we leave now we will reach the kibbutz under cover of darkness. We will park at the furniture store on the east side of the kibbutz and from there slip out through the orchards, climb the fence, and walk a few hundred metres into Tulkarim." He paused, looking thoughtful. "We will have to be careful of the kibbutz security team and change into Arab-style clothes as soon as we are over the fence. Dani, Shimon and I will have to do most of the talking. Your Arabic might not pass."

Fortunately, I had in my wardrobe some Arab *keffiyas** – souvenirs from an undercover exercise completed years ago. I also had a collection of jackets more suitable for Tulkarim than our old army-issue down *dubons*. Without further ado, we packed our

---

* *Arabic: Arab head-dress.*

changes of clothing into unmarked plastic bags and set off for the kibbutz.

Ten kilometres from the Beit Lid junction on the Netanya border, we arrived at the crossroad turn-off to Kibbutz Yad Chana, only five hundred metres from the entrance to Tulkarim, and almost on top of the army roadblock. We turned left and, a few hundred metres later, turned right into the unguarded entrance to the kibbutz.

Parking our car between the furniture store and the main kibbutz parking lot – where with any luck it would go unnoticed for some time – we slipped off to the nearby orchards, clutching our plastic bags in the gathering darkness. Undetected, we soon came to the dirt road bordering the security fence. Swiftly changing our clothing so that we resembled Tulkarim Arabs with our jackets and keffiyas, we hid the plastic bags with our normal clothing in a pile of brush-wood cuttings.

"Now comes the really dangerous part," joked Shimon. "If the kibbutz security people see us dressed like this and climbing the fence, they might think we are trying to get in and not out. We wouldn't be the first to be hit by warning shots."

Suddenly we saw the headlights of a jeep approaching us, and ducked down into the undergrowth. Pulled up dangerously close to our hiding place, the jeep stopped and two burly *kibbutzniks** alighted, heading straight for us.

---

* *Hebrew: Members of a kibbutz.*

Chapter 5

As I burrowed into the undergrowth, I prayed that my friends had also seen the rapidly approaching heavyweights, and were making sure that they were well hidden. Closer and closer, the two security guards moved heavily towards us. Not a word was uttered by either of them. Their very silence added to my nervous tension.

Suddenly, the larger of the two spoke. "Can't see anyone here – I told you it was just your imagination."

"I'm still sure that I saw something," said his companion, "let's get the dogs here; they'll know for sure."

"OK – you go get them. I'll stay here and make sure your imaginary terrorists don't escape."

"Right! I'm off then," said the first man. Suiting his actions to his words, he sprang into the jeep and drove back towards the guardhouse.

None of us wanted to harm a fellow Israeli, but we knew that when the dogs arrived we would be discovered. We had to act fast; to hell with the fallout. From the corner of my eye, I saw Gadir slither silently behind the big security man. Kneeling behind him, he beckoned to me.

Realizing what Gadir was suggesting, I rose up slightly, and from a kneeling position launched myself violently at the *kibbutznik*'s knees. Before he could catch a glimpse of me or even realise what was happening, he was tumbling backwards into the undergrowth near Shimon's hiding place.

Shimon hit him swiftly on the base of the skull with a large stone – just hard enough to knock him out for a few minutes. Immediately, we ran for the fence and threw ourselves over it, running for cover in the nearby *wadi** before he could come to and see us.

"*Ya-allah*, that was close," said Gadir.

"Too damned close," I agreed. "What a way to start off our mission."

"Dani, you're right, I'm afraid," said Shimon, "but not to worry, there's no way he saw you. The evening's dark and cloudy. With a bit of luck, he might even think it was a wild boar; there's a lot around here, you know."

Comforted by the idea, I agreed. "I did hit him very low, below the knees. He fell back hard," I reflected.

"Yes," said Gadir, "it was just the right place to hit him, and the right height. He will most likely come around thinking he hit his head on the rocks."

"Hopefully," I added, "that'll convince his friend that what he saw was only a wild pig. After all, we're on the other side of the fence now. We won't be giving them any problems."

We all knew that the real danger was only just beginning. We were on the wrong side of the West Bank, and despite our disguises, the smallest mistake could give us away. If we were discovered by Hamas terrorists, death was certain. And it would surely come as a relief after questioning by torture.

By now, the last traces of light had disappeared from the sky, and the new moon provided no help at all in finding our way. "Best that we rest up where we are," said Shimon, "we can make our way into the town after daybreak. When the workers come into the fields, it should be easy to blend into the scene."

"Good idea," I said. "Let's lie down there in the *wadi** where no can see us." It had been a long day, and the prospect of rest was appealing. I headed for some big clumps of reed in the dried-up river bed I had pointed out to the others. "These will make a good hiding place, and provide us with bedding too," I said as I began bending reeds to form a makeshift bed.

"I'm ready to keel over," Shimon replied, "but only two of us can sleep at a time. We'll have to take two-hour shifts standing guard." Gadir volunteered for the first spell of guard duty. Shimon would be next, and then it would be my turn.

* Hebrew: *Dried up river bed.*

No sooner had I managed to get to sleep than I felt Gadir shaking me awake. As I blinked into the darkness, I saw that Shimon had already woken and was crouching, utterly still, facing west. There, in the direction that Gadir was silently pointing, I saw silhouetted faintly against the skyline three Arabs hooded in *keffiyas*, heading towards our hiding place. With the night's blackness and their head wraps it was impossible to identify them, but there was no doubt that they were coming from Tulkarim. And if they spotted us…

To my alarm, Gadir suddenly stood up to confront them. "Don't go that way," he said in Arabic, "there is a security alert on the kibbutz – they nearly caught us. We just managed to get away. We are waiting for them to go back to bed before we try again. You can wait here with us if you like."

"Allah looks after his own," said the leader. "Thank you, my brother, but we will go a little further and get in through the fence near the turkey pens. We have far to go tonight."

"Allah be with you, *habibi*,*" said Gadir. "Go in peace and return safely." They headed away from us, and soon disappeared from sight.

"Car thieves," whispered Gadir. "They use the kibbutz as a way of bypassing the roadblocks to Netanya. They most likely thought we were in the same business and wanted to get there before us," he went on. "Go back to sleep, I will call you when it's your turn."

I took the next shift, and after two uneventful hours handed over to Shimon. When I lay down again, my bed of reeds felt almost comfortable, and also much softer than before.

Shimon woke me at daybreak, far more gently than was his custom. Fingers to his lips, he had his hand on my shoulder, holding me down. There was a horrified look on Gadir's face.

"Don't move!" said Shimon, very softly, "and don't talk. You are lying on a snake." Frozen with fright, I suddenly realised why my bed had felt so comfortable. For the first time ever, I blessed my few kilo's of extra weight. I was pinning the snake down with my XXL-sized body.

The reptile was now trying to wriggle beneath me, and was

---

* Arabic: My friend.

probably as frightened as I was. The problem was how to get up without giving it a chance to strike. The longer I lay there, the more chance it had of getting free. I could already feel its body desperately twitching, wriggling for freedom liked a hooked fish.

For once, Gadir was at a loss for words. The Bedouin, living in the wilds as they do, have an inherent fear of reptiles, especially vipers. His fear was no comfort to me; from the glimpse I'd had of the snake's mottled green and black body, that was exactly what I was lying on. The Palestinian viper is the most poisonous of all the snakes found in Israel. It is also the fastest.

Shimon, as usual, kept his cool. Taking out his sheath knife, he shoved the flat of the blade between my back and the snake's writhing body. "Dani, you're going to have to help me. I can't cut the snake just anywhere; wounded it will be even more vicious. Somehow, we will have to find its head."

In spite of the cold dawn air, I was slick with sweat as I pressed my back even harder into the twisting length of the snake, turning my neck and head to catch a glimpse of either its head or its tail. I had no success. "I can't," I mouthed to the others. "It's taking all I have to just keep him pinned down. He's fighting harder and harder and I can't see a thing."

Gadir was now lying on the ground next to me, finding it equally impossible to locate the viper's head. "Hold out for one more minute, Dani, we must try something else," he said softly. "You take Dani's legs, Shimon, and I'll take his ankles. We must throw him as far away as we can. On the count of three!"

"One. Two. Three!" Suddenly I felt myself flying through the air, landing with a thud just three metres away. I heard Shimon laugh, "There he goes!"

Looking in the direction he was pointing, I saw the long grass quivering in the reptile's wake as it made its escape.

"That was a big one, Dani," said a shaken Gadir, "definitely over a metre long." I had been very, very lucky to escape with my life.

"Thanks!" I breathed with relief. "*Chevra**! That was too close for comfort. Let's get out of here before his mate arrives." So saying, I headed rapidly out of the *wadi*, treading as carefully as I could.

* *Hebrew: My friends.*

Chapter 6

Tulkarim! An Arab city only 16 kilometres from Netanya, it had been inhabited since Roman times. Today, with a population of about 20,000, it was one of the larger towns on the West Bank. Captured from Jordan by Israel in 1967's Six-Day War, it had, since the Intifada, become a centre of Hamas activity.

Looking at the town, silhouetted as it was against the rising sun, I remembered a time – not so long ago, really – when it was a favoured shopping destination for bargain hunters from Netanya. Now, any Israeli visiting Tulkarim did so at the risk of his life.

Built on a series of hills, the town was dominated by the domes and minarets of the local mosques. In contrast to the dawn vista, which painted a picture of ancient beauty, seemingly straight out of the *Arabian Nights*, the details revealed as the sun rose higher into the sky portrayed the ravages of globalisation. Large satellite dishes marred the tops of the tallest buildings, and a veritable forest of TV antennae in varying states of disarray rose from nearly every house.

Slowly and carefully, we made our way to the northern outskirts of the town. The best way – perhaps the only way – for us to locate Jibril was to join in the gossip of the coffee shops where most of the town's unemployed men gathered during the day. There, we would ask a few questions, hoping to be accepted by the locals as harmless visitors from Gaza. Visitors seeking a long-lost cousin.

Walking through the town, the visible scars of the Intifada deepened my gloomy mood. The walls of the buildings skirting the town were held together by cracked and crumbling plaster. Stone-walled dwellings, looking much as they had when built at the turn of the century, exuded the dignity of their age. The stoic way in which they held their ground against the encroachment of the more modern buildings deepened my nostalgia for Tulkarim's brighter days.

The shops held very little to entice buyers to enter, and their keepers stood hopelessly in empty doorways, looking onto roads densely pocked with potholes. The streets seemed eerily quiet compared to the perennial traffic jams of Netanya. Small boys rode two-wheeled donkey carts carelessly, with no danger to either themselves or others. There were very few women on the street; for long stretches of road, the drifting fragrance of baking pita and frying vegetables was the only trace of their existence. Now and then, a black-clad figure would hurry past, eyes averted, hair covered by a *hijab*.*

"You can see why Hamas has succeeded here," whispered Shimon, "these people would snatch at the smallest hope." People here clearly had little to lose, and Hamas's promises of a better future were a lot more than they got from the fat cats of Fatah,** who were busy lining their own pockets while poverty deepened on the streets.

Economic gloom notwithstanding, there was a certain strange beauty to the town. Here and there, the dusty streets were overlooked by three- and four-storey buildings with arched arabesque windows and porticos. Between one crouching building and another, one suddenly came across orchards, where brilliantly hued bougainvilleas ran wild, their purple and orange blossoms blazing. Elsewhere, the occasional lone jacaranda tree sprinkled brilliant blue petals onto the road below. The wintery sun quickly muted their rich colour, leaving scraggly carpets of heat-whitened blossoms littering the street.

Plodding our way up the steep hills, we sought out a likely coffee house. On one of the high sidewalks five men were seated on wooden stools around a small low table covered with tiny coffee cups. No commercial enterprise this; just a few friends and neighbours, gossiping away. On seeing us, they stopped talking, and watched suspiciously as we passed by. Obviously, in this neighbourhood, strangers were not welcome.

* *Headscarf worn by religious Muslim women.*
** *Ruling party in Palestine.*

As we continued on our way, I sensed someone moving behind us. A cold shiver rippled down my spine, and a heavy foreboding settled on my shoulders, but when I looking over my shoulder, I saw no-one. Noticing my cautious demeanour, Shimon raised his eyebrows.

"Did you see something, Dani?" he whispered as he strode on, keeping a steady gait. I hadn't. Now Gadir looked across at me, curiously.

"I don't know... it was just a feeling," I muttered, keeping pace with the others. Feeling slightly abashed by my sudden attack of nerves, I dismissed the spell, laughing apologetically, "That snake this morning must have put me on edge. Either that or my imagination." Just then, I spotted a coffee house. "Hey, what's that up ahead?" I said, relieved to escape my friends' scrutiny.

On the next block was just the sort of place we were looking for. With 40 percent unemployment in the town, the wooden tables and chairs were teeming with men who had little else to do – a crowd we could melt into without drawing unwanted attention. Surrounded by noisy chatter and passing traffic, it was unlikely my halting Arabic would be noticed.

Finding a vacant table, we sat down and scanned the room. Almost immediately, a waiter appeared, bringing cups and an old brass pot before we even had time to order. From its long, curved spout, he poured us cups of sweet, thick Turkish coffee. Again without our asking, a plate of baklava appeared on the table. We refused his offer of a *hookah* pipe,* making ours virtually the only table without a bubbling *hookah* to share.

This was the first time that we had eaten since rising at dawn, and the coffee and over-sweet pastries hit me like a shot of adrenaline, a rush that made me made me almost dizzy. Our coffee pot emptied fast, as did our plates, and the waiter reappeared at our table as if radar-guided. "*Shukra,*** my brother," Shimon thanked him, "may Allah be with you for your service to weary travelers. Perhaps you can give us even more help? We will not be ungrateful. Can you, by chance, also help us in our quest? We are from Gaza and strange to your beautiful city."

---

* *Originally from Hindi: Water pipe.*
** *Arabic: Thank you.*

"You see," said Gadir. "A friend who died recently charged us on his death bed to find one from Tulkarim to whom he owed money. He gave to us many dinars to pay back the debt on his behalf, so that he could join the righteous in Paradise, free of earthly debts."

At the mention of money, the waiter's eyes lit up with barely concealed avarice. "I know many, many people," he replied, as he calculated what might be in it for him, "tell me, please, if you are willing, his name. Thus, I too, Allah permitting, can earn merit in Paradise by assisting you in your worthy cause."

"His name is Jibril Tirawin," said Shimon. "We were told that he had lost his job recently, and was forced to work for the rich Jews in Netanya at a starvation wage. If you can help us reach him, you will not find us ungrateful. Even more importantly, Allah will bless you for aiding a brother in distress."

Shimon went on to introduce himself as Mussa and the two of us as Ebrahim and Gadir. The waiter, who informed us in his obsequious manner that his name was Suleiman, instructed us to return in a few hours time. He planned to slip out during his midday break, and promised to have news for us once he had done the rounds with his contacts.

Leaving the coffee house, I once more felt the creeping sensation that someone was watching us. Looking around, I could see nothing out of place, and cursed the morning's events that had turned me into a quivering wreck for the day. I comforted myself with the thought that it was hardly strange to feel uneasy, considering who we were and where we were walking.

"Now what?" I asked the others.

Shimon's usually carefree face looked tense. "I don't think we should ask any more questions for now," he said. "I noticed a sudden hush at the nearby tables when we mentioned Jibril's name. It might have been my imagination, but I got the impression he was known there. Yet no-one offered us help in our search. It is worrying that we have drawn so much attention to ourselves." His brow was heavy. "We must return for Suleiman's information as soon after midday as possible, or there is no way we will be done with our investigations before nightfall," he continued, with a frown. "Maybe we should give up altogether," he said finally.

"What?!" replied Gadir, "we have not only sworn to revenge Gidon's death, we also have a mission to complete. If Jibril is involved in acquiring a tactical nuclear weapon for Hamas, we cannot give up. Whatever the risk, we must do all we can to prevent that from happening!"

"*Ein brerah** – no choice, we must return," I said.

Not to be outdone in courage by me – the most easily spooked of the three of us – Shimon summoned up his usual, unruffled persona. "We are not women, to be frightened of imaginary fears," said Shimon. "I've pointed out our choices because it wouldn't hurt to lower our profile. There's no chance of achieving our mission if we are unlucky enough to be caught here before we have found Jibril."

"I have the same feeling that we've caught the attention of the wrong people," I replied, "But Gadi's right; we have to continue at all costs. Against the threat of a nuclear holocaust, all risks are acceptable." So saying, I looked once more over my shoulder, and again saw nothing unusual.

"Agreed," said Shimon. "Let's go back the way we came in and detour to the main road. This neighborhood is too quiet; people seem to know each other and I feel like an obvious intruder."

Gadir, seemingly immune to the anxiety that had infected myself and Shimon, broke the tension. "Right, Dani, let us go. Perhaps we can pick up some bargains at the local stores while we are waiting," he joked, setting off down the hill without waiting for a reply.

Shimon and I smiled in spite of ourselves and followed his lead. Going down the hill, we passed on our left the small table of coffee drinkers we had seen on our way up an hour ago. From the corner of my eye, I noticed that there had been one change: there were now only four men at the table. Once again, they seemed to be eyeing us with more interest than was warranted for mere passers by.

As we turned the corner towards the main road, I spoke up. "Is it my imagination, or did those four we just passed pay more attention to us than necessary?"

* *Hebrew: No option.*

"I also sensed something," said Shimon. Gadir nodded his agreement.

"You were right, Shimon. Our profile is too high. We will need to disappear into the crowds in the marketplace." Gadir glanced around, getting his bearings. "Follow me, I know just where to go. Let us talk as little as possible; your Arabic, Dani, is too formal. It will raise even more suspicion."

Walking swiftly down the hill towards the marketplace, I kept trying to look around me without being too obvious about it. Still I saw nothing unusual, which made the sudden blow to the back of my head even more surprising. Sinking to my knees, I felt yet another blow ram my skull, and the whole world went black.

Chapter 7

When I came to I found myself lying on the ground with my wrists and ankles tied so tightly that my hands and feet were senseless, as if they had been amputated. Peering into the dark, I could see the bodies of Shimon and Gadir trussed up nearby. All three of us had been roped to a rusty iron bar set into the stonework of the room, our hands tied up behind us. Our backs were literally against the wall.

A little light filtered into the darkness around us through a steel grating set close to the ceiling on the opposite side of the room. The whole area was dank, and water dripped softly from condensation on the stone ceiling above us. We had obviously been taken to one of the old stone houses that looked so charming as we had wandered through the town earlier in the day.

Never before had I felt so completely helpless – unable even to lift a hand to wipe away the blood that was leaking into my right eye from somewhere on my head. It seemed that I had been the first to regain consciousness. Both Gadir and Shimon were motionless, their eyes closed. Gadir seemed to be relatively unharmed, but Shimon was badly battered, one eye and lip black and swollen, his right cheek covered in what I could only assume was blood.

There seemed to be no one else in the room, which seemed, on closer inspection, to be either a cellar or possibly a sort of semi-basement. This would account for the damp walls and ceiling, and also for the eerie silence, which was punctuated only by the occasional plink of dripping water.

My whole body ached. We were tied up in so contorted a way that even if we were freed we would be too stiff to make an escape. Fortunately, my mind was still functioning fairly well, and I tried in vain to work out how, despite our military and undercover training, we had been surprised by our attackers and overpowered so quickly and effortlessly.

Unable to see my watch – uncertain whether it was even still on my arm – I had no idea how long we had been lying in the cellar, or what the time now was. One clue was that the light coming in through the grating seemed to be growing dimmer, meaning that the early winter evening would soon be upon us. In a short while, we would be in complete darkness.

Straining my ears, I thought that I could hear mutters issuing from Shimon, who seemed to be coming round. "Can you hear me?" I whispered, and was surprised hear a reply, not from Shimon but from Gadir.

"Be careful what you say, Dani. I am sure the walls have ears," he breathed, so softly that I could barely hear him. As I nodded in response, pain wrenched through me, reminding me just where I had been hit.

Shimon was now also conscious, adding in a whisper: "The less we say, the better. Stay silent – we may learn more that way. Just play it cool." Trained in survival techniques as we were, there was little to be done but to try and recover our strength. Relaxing our minds and bodies would speed up the process of natural healing, which would help us to recover as fast as possible without medical assistance.

Knowing that in our present position there was little we could do to escape, we all three tried to wriggle into the most comfortable positions we could find and closed our eyes, trying to clear our minds. I must have fallen asleep somehow, and was awakened by the sound of a door being opened. I awoke to see light flooding through the open doorway into the near-blackness of our cell. Silhouetted in the doorway was a man armed with what looked like a Kalashnikov assault rifle, his *keffiya* headscarf almost completely covering his face. His frame – tall and well built – was particularly menacing from my prone position as he made his way into the room.

"I know exactly who you are!" he barked in local Arabic, "So don't waste my time with your stupid lies! When I ask questions, I will expect truthful answers!" So saying, he kicked me twice, painfully, in the ribs. It was obvious that in our helpless position we were completely at his mercy.

Knowing that my stilted Arabic would give us away, Gadir quickly intervened. "We are simple travelers, *Effendi*.* All we want is to pay back a debt of honour for one who is now dead." Hearing this, our captor turned his attention away from me and kicked Gadir even harder than he had kicked me.

"You lying dog! We know that you three were at the hotel in Netanya. We have been waiting for you for the last two days! We want to know who you are and why you risked your lives with this foolish journey."

I suddenly realised what had happened. Mario Hajaj, manager of the Surf Crest Hotel, must have caught wind of Gadir's questioning about Jibril, and become suspicious when he did not turn up for work the next day – particularly after Shimon and I had sat in the lounge throughout Gadir's first shift, leaving when it ended. He knew we had security connections, and must also have known something about Jibril's background. As a sweetener to preserve his good standing with the Tulkarim crime families, he had probably got word out to them to be on the lookout for three strangers asking about Jibril.

Looking meaningfully at my two friends, I sensed that they had reached the same conclusion. But before our captor could question us further, a shout rang out from above. "Yussef! Jibril wants you up here! We need to talk!" Hearing this, the interrogator fairly sprang to attention, turned on his heel and left the room. We heard him bounding up a staircase.

"You see," said Shimon softly, "we've already learnt a lot. They don't know exactly who we are, Yussef is one of at least three gang members, and Jibril seems to be his boss. At last we seem to have found the man who murdered Gidon."

"Yes, we have gathered good information," whispered Gadir in return, "but if to know more means we must stay here, I would prefer to sacrifice more knowledge and get out of this rat-infested cellar. We may know more, but we can do nothing until we are able to leave." Gadir's words drew my attention, for the first time, to the large, furry rodents lurking in the far corner of the room, their movements only just visible in the faint light. Helpless as we were, we would be at their mercy if they decided to pursue a

---

* *Arabic: My Lord.*

more varied meat diet. The thought gave me a crazy, last-ditch escape plan. Given enough time and a little luck, it might just work.

"Shimon!" I whispered urgently, "can you wriggle a little closer to me?" As he did so, shimmying along the rail, I told him to bend his head close to my wrists. "There! That's it!" I cried as he did so, hitting his injured cheek as he tried to lean over. "What the hell?! Are you completely *meshuggah*!*" he exclaimed, as the blood started pouring from the re-opened wound. "Maybe, but if this works you'll still thank me. Trust me – keep your head right there." His blood flowed freely down my arms, soaking my hands and their bonds.

"OK, you can move back to where you were," I said once the blood began to slow. Both of you, keep quiet. Don't move; don't whisper."

Once more, the only sound was the slow dripping of water. What felt like hours later – though it may only have been a few minutes – I heard the scrabbling sound of rats' claws venturing closer to us. One of the largest rodents hurried nearer and nearer, until he suddenly disappeared from my sight. Almost at once, the others gained confidence and followed him behind me toward my bound wrists, slippery with poor Shimon's blood.

Quickly, using all my remaining strength, I tensed my forearms like a body-builder, preparing myself for the very last form of torture I would have anticipated at the hands of our captors. As the rat pack found their target, I gritted my teeth, staying silent and immobile as they began to gnaw.

Sweating and grimacing from the pain, I withstood it until I felt the rope loosening around my wrists. The rats had gnawed through the bloody ropes binding my arms, biting into the skin of my hands and wrists in the process. But the pain had been worthwhile – my hands were free. As the feeling returned to my limbs, I grabbed the nearest rat, swung him by his long tail, and threw his body as hard as I could into the far corner of the room.

There, thankfully, his limp body was at once set upon by his friends. Deserting me for an easier meal.

---

* *Hebrew: Crazy.*

Chapter 8

Even with my hands free, it still took time to get my fingers working freely enough to untie my ankles. Every agonizing minute, I expected to hear our captors returning to the cellar.

As fast as I could, I untied Shimon's and Gadir's hands, leaving them to untie their own feet. I had barely finished, when we heard the sound of someone descending the creaking wooden stairs. "Slump back!" whispered Gadir, "keep your hands behind you!"

Suddenly, the darkness gave way to the faint light of a flickering torch as Yussef returned to inspect us. "Water!" muttered Shimon, "For the love of Allah give us water, we are dying of thirst."

Yussef kicked him in the ribs and laughed, "Drink your own piss, you dogs! You'll get nothing from me until I hear who you really are and why you're here." Then, with all the force he had, he kicked each of us in turn. I thought I heard a rib snap in my chest.

He continued, without a pause, kicking fiercely at each of us in turn, as he exclaimed: "This is nothing compared to what you will get, you filthy flea-covered dogs, if I don't hear what I want from you!"

"I talk, *Effendi*, I talk," Shimon barely whispered.

"Talk up! Louder!" yelled Yussef, and kicked him again. Shimon's voice went even softer and he could barely be heard as he babbled, seemingly delirious. Yussef grew even angrier. "Talk up! Talk up! I must hear what you say before you get water!" Now, Shimon spoke even more softly. He seemed to be making sense, but his voice was almost inaudible.

Cursing angrily, Yussef dropped to his knees and put his left ear close to Shimon's mouth, trying desperately to hear his fading words. Suddenly, Shimon was galvanised back to life, grabbing Yussef's neck in a choke hold with his freed right arm. The man could barely be heard as he gasped for breath.

Now it was my turn to act. Lurching for Yussef's filthy *keffiya*, I forced it into his mouth, effectively gagging him. I used his worn leather belt to secure the gag. It felt good to get my own back at last, but Yussef wasn't giving up without a fight. Weak as he was, Shimon managed to keep hold of Yussef's throat as he thrashed about. I got another boot in the chest during the melee, and, throwing my body over his legs, I once again blessed those excess kilograms as the kicking slowed down and stopped.

Yussef's body was vainly twitching as he tried to escape our combined grasp. Once Gadir had untied his own feet – a quicker process as his hands, loosened for the duration of our struggle with Yussef, had regained the life they needed to work fast – we now had our chance. We had more than enough rope to shackle the gagged Yussef to the wall bar. That done, Shimon pressed his index finger on the nerves of the man's neck, and seconds later Yussef collapsed into unconsciousness.

"Right! One down and at least two to go," muttered Shimon, but I knew that we had only two relatively fit and able players on our team. I was dizzy and trying desperately to hold onto consciousness. This, together with the kicks I had taken to the ribs, meant I would be of little use until I had a chance to get my act back together. I put my hands to my head, trying to fend off another wave of unconsciousness. The blows to my head had definitely taken their toll, draining my remaining strength.

Shimon could see what was happening. "You lie down, Dani. Just play dead – you won't find it too hard. Leave the next bit to Gadi and me," he told me. So saying, he quickly tore a strip from his own shirt and changed it for the keffiya we had used to gag Yussef. He then stripped off and donned the man's shirt. With the keffiya on his head, it was difficult to see who was who in the dark.

"That was easy; now for the difficult part," he whispered, "Gadi, you're our resident source of bright ideas. How are we going get information out of Jibril and still get out of here alive?"

Gadir thought for a few moments, "Not easy; not easy at all," he mused, "I am certain he is Hamas – they would gratefully die as martyrs assured of Paradise rather than submit to us and surrender their secrets. To get out of here will be easy, but that is not what we came for! To simply escape, without finding out if he killed Gidon and what was behind it all? No, that is not what we came here for." This was the longest statement I had ever heard from Gadir, and the absence of his usual comforting, light-hearted tone was noticeable. If nothing else, a joke-free Gadir was a definite indication of just how deep the shit we had got ourselves into was.

"Give me a few minutes, Shimon. I will think of a good plan. In the meantime, Dani will have some time to recover. He is going to need his strength."

Time, however, was a luxury we would have to do without. A light now appeared from above, and we heard someone descending the stairs, calling angrily: "Yussef, what in hell's name is taking so long? What – are you offering them coffee and baklava, and a nice chat? No, no. I will show you how it's done."

Chapter 9

The creaking of the wooden stairs drew closer, and with no time to talk, I played dead, leaving my friends to navigate this new dilemma. Gadir spoke up as a gigantic man entered the doorway, his face hidden by a black hood.

"Mercy, *Effendi*, take mercy on an old man. Only spare me and I will talk., My one friend is dead and the other will join him soon. I have no one to betray!"

"Talk! Talk, you dog," muttered Shimon, turning his face towards Gadir and away from the newcomer.

"No time for women's chatter!" yelled the hooded giant, pushing Shimon violently away. "Don't you know Jibril will be back soon? How will we look if we have no answers for him?!" and taking a shining knife from a sheath on his belt he pressed its edge into Gadir's throat.

Time froze. The man had turned the tables on us despite all the progress we had made. Gadir was lying helpless with a knife at his throat, and Shimon had been hurled into a corner, too far away to act without endangering our friend. That left me, light-headed and verging on unconsciousness, as our only hope.

Even in the weak light, the blade of the knife shone, filling me with dread. One false move and the knife would slash Gadir's throat. The hooded giant would have no difficulty in dispatching Shimon and I soon afterwards.

Only surprise could help us. If I could divert the man's attention for just a moment we might have a chance.

"Open fire – fire at will!" I screamed in Hebrew. The giant's head jerked towards the staircase. Shimon, who had been silently advancing from the corner, threw himself at the man as Gadir twisted the knife and heaved it blindly towards the man's chest.

Wounded as he was, the huge man put up a massive fight, grabbing the knife and lunging at Shimon. Fresh blood from a wound in my friend's stomach joined the congealed blood on the floor, which became slippery as we struggled to subdue our enemy. Shimon was weakening rapidly, and even with three of us against him the giant had the better of the fight.

Hungry, their blood lust aroused, the rats took courage and scuttled closer, looking for a chance to feed. They were to come to our aid once again: weaponless and very weak, I gathered my remaining strength, seized a rat by its long tail, and swung it like a slingshot at the big man's face. The terrified rat clawed at his bearded face, blinding him with its sharp claws.

Now, only Gadir was fit to fight, and stabbing the giant repeatedly he overcame him with a final slash to the neck. The knife must have severed an artery: blood exploded out of the wound in a black fountain, and with a last, horrible gurgle, the man was finally silent.

Shimon, too, was desperately wounded. The slash to his stomach was deep and jagged, and he was in a very bad way. Using the dead giant's knife, I cut my shirt to pieces and tried to staunch the flow of blood from Shimon's body.

"Gadi, we have to get out of here fast," I urged, "without proper medical help, he has no chance."

Shimon overheard and even in his weakened state objected violently. "No way, Dani," he gasped, "you can't – abandon – the mission. You must go on – with – or – without me. Too much is – at stake!"

"He is right," said Gadir, "Shimon's is only one life. Somehow, we must catch Jibril and discover whether a nuclear plot against Israel exists. If it does, attack and counterattack could engulf whole nations. Our lives are small in comparison." While I agreed with Gadi, this seemed no time for one of his lengthy declarations of self sacrifice for the greater good.

"Fine. Maybe we can save everyone. We'll wait for Jibril, capture him and smuggle him back to Netanya to interrogate him," I said. "I don't know how we're going to do that, but at least back home Shimon can get some help." Gadir didn't argue. I left the planning up to him.

With no more to be said, Gadir and I somehow managed to get a rapidly weakening Shimon up the wooden staircase to the ground floor. And not a moment too soon. As we neared the front door, it opened before us. Here was the man we had sought for so long: dark faced, with hawk-like features and a trimmed beard, his piercing eyes a startling blue. His head was covered in a black-and-white checked *keffiya*. Though he was clearly younger than us, his presence alone told us this was one of the few, dangerous men who virtually radiate power.

With the build of a welterweight boxer, Jibril would be no easy match. Fortunately, surprise was on our side – though in honesty we were almost as startled as he at our sudden meeting.

"What are you doing up here, Yussef? And where is Ibrahim?" He obviously thought that Shimon, still wearing Yussef's *keffiya*, was one of his sidekicks, and before he had a chance to realise his mistake both Gadir and I leapt on him. Or rather, Gadir leapt and I fell more than pounced on his right shoulder.

Two tired, middle-aged ex-paratroopers were no match for a fit younger man, and we had no hope of overcoming him until Shimon gathered up the last of his strength to throw Yussef's dagger at Jibril. Aimed at the chest, it missed badly and thudded into the back of Jibril's left knee just as he put his weight on the leg to swing a looping right punch at my jaw. The punch landed and we both collapsed. Now Gadir was the only one on his feet. Quick thinking, as usual, he threw himself on Jibril and, grasping the man's ears, slammed his head on the stone floor: once, and then again. Unconscious, he lay limply beside me as I struggled to regain my senses.

"Wake up, Dani! Wake up!" Gadi urged, his hand shaking my shoulder. "I need your help right away. We have to tie up Jibril and help Shimon, and I cannot do both."

Somehow, I got to my feet and, looking at Jibril, I realised just how lucky we had been. But Shimon's last plunge with the knife had re-opened his stomach wound, and he was bleeding badly. His normally rosy face was deathly white. Quickly rebinding his wound, I felt for his pulse, which was barely fluttering. His forehead felt as cold as ice. Once again, my friend Shimon had come to our aid, but by saving our lives it seemed he might well have lost his own.

Chapter 10

A full day must have passed since we first entered Tulkarim – once again, dawn was breaking. As I scouted cautiously through the door of the house – open barely a crack – I saw once more the minarets silhouetted against the rising sun. Lights were already coming on in some of the nearby apartments as early risers began the day. If we were to get out unobserved, now was definitely the time.

We had some real problems to overcome, though. Shimon was helpless – unable even to walk – and Jibril, bound and gagged as he was, would have to be kept out of sight until we were well outside the town entrance. The obvious solution was to borrow a car. Leaving Gadir to guard Jibril and tend as best as he could to Shimon, I set out to find one.

It was easier said than done. Somehow, our basic army training had neglected to offer a course in car theft, and I found that none of the cars parked in the neighbourhood had been left unlocked, with keys left conveniently in the ignition. In American movies, this never seemed to be a problem.

If car theft was out, then car hijacking seemed to be the answer. I looked desperately for an early riser on his way to work. No one in sight. Suddenly, I had one of my rare flashes of brilliance. Running as fast as I could back to the stone house, I hissed, "Gadi, is there a phone in the house?" There was.

"Great! Call an ambulance – as quickly as possible. The Red Crescent work 24 hours a day, and at this time of the morning they'll be here in minutes!"

"Fine Dani – but how do we explain all the stab wounds? They will call the police as soon as they see us."

"Trust me, Gadi, they won't. Leave it to me!"

Quick on the uptake as usual, Gadir wasted no time. The emergency numbers hadn't changed since the last Israeli re-occupation, less than a year previously, and only moments later an ambulance pulled up outside, its siren piercing the morning's stillness. As neighbours began emerging in their nightclothes and running over to see what had happened, I cursed emergency vehicles the world over for their obsession with blaring sirens. The dawn silence of the street gave way to a commotion reminiscent of the Netanya *shouk* as everyone competed to shout advice and find out just what had happened. My plan to hijack the ambulance was foiled. There seemed no way we could now escape with both our wounded comrade and the unconscious captive we had hidden behind the door.

Seeing my helpless expression, Gadir came to the rescue. "Keep out of the way!" he shouted, "We have a man dying of AIDS here. His brother stabbed him to save the family honour and there is infected blood everywhere." All of a sudden, the crowd evaporated, although a few still hovered at a safe distance, eager to squeeze out the last drops of the tragedy to retail later to their friends and relations.

From the expressions on their faces it was clear that the Red Crescent paramedics were equally unenthusiastic at the idea of encountering HIV-positive blood – although, to their credit, they had stood their ground. Gadir took advantage of the situation. Adopting a pious tone, he declared: "They are our family members; we will put them in the ambulance to spare you the danger. One of you sit with me and tell me what to do, and my cousin will sit up front with the driver." The two men were only too happy to agree. Once we had loaded Shimon and Jibril, strapped to stretchers, into the back, I got in with the driver, leaving Gadir to attend to his colleague.

I waited only for the ambulance to leave the immediate neighbourhood before I took Ibrahim's knife from my belt and held it to the driver's throat. "Now listen to me and listen well. Your life depends on it!" I hissed. "If you do as I say I swear I will let you live, but one fault and I will cut your throat like a dog!"

Too scared to reply, he mumbled an affirmation. I could feel him trembling with fright as I grasped his shoulder. "Drive to the gates of the city, and stop there," I instructed. "I will tell you what to do when we get there."

To be honest, I wasn't sure myself. As soon as we exited Tulkarim, we would be stopped at the guardhouse of the Israeli border police, who manned a permanent roadblock about a hundred meters outside Tulkarim on the main road to Netanya. At present there was no order of closure on the Palestinian self-rule area, so we were free to travel, but the police would undoubtedly stop us and check out our vehicle. This would elicit way too many questions to answer briefly, and the tough Druse border police were notorious for taking action first and asking questions later.

By the time we reached the decorative metal arch at the Tulkarim boundary, I still had no idea how we were going to get through the police barrier without the delay – and very probably discomfort – of a police interrogation.

As the ambulance stopped, a small boy came up to the window. He and his friends spent their days on the outskirts of Tulkarim, selling cheap *hookahs* and artifacts to passing tourists. Undeterred by the ambulance – and too short to see my knife at the driver's throat – he diligently plied his trade.

"Buy this *hookah* from me, *Effendi*. Very cheap! Very good! The mayor himself bought one last week!" Undaunted by my frown and curt shake of the head, he pressed on. "Please don't say no!" he pleaded forcefully, "I beg of you, consider my other bargains! My *sheik*,* I have the best selection in all of Tulkarim!"

In spite of myself, I glanced out of the window at the mat he had spread on the dusty ground, on which his selection of junk merchandise was carefully arranged. Suddenly, I caught sight of something that might just help us.

*Arabic: Leader.

Chapter 11

There on the mat, almost covered by a cheap tablecloth, was a cellular phone. I pointed to it – "There, that might just interest me, if the price is right."

"*Effendi*, that is not for sale," the boy replied, "it is my very own phone which I use in my business."

If the situation had not been so desperate, I would have burst out laughing. There was no way that he could have bought the phone legally; it must have been stolen and difficult to pass off as merchandise since the buyer would want access to the cellphone network.

"I need the phone to call the hospital in Israel," I said. "We have a dying patient who cannot be treated here, and we urgently need to arrange with Laniado hospital in Netanya that they take him without problems."

"In that case, *Effendi*, you can use my phone for your call. There will be no charge," he replied earnestly.

"I also want to buy that tablecloth. How much is it?"

"Only 10 shekels, *Effendi*."

"Fine, I'll take it. But I only have a fifty shekel note and no small change. Can you change it for me?"

His face fell. Fifty shekels would be a whole day's takings for him – certainly not an amount he would be carrying on him.

"I'll run for change, *Effendi*," he declared with determination.

"Well, hurry. We cannot wait." As the boy sped off, giving me the time and space I needed, I threw the 50 shekel note out of the window as a reward on his return. The use of his phone was priceless.

Quickly, I dialled Meyer Jephet at the Shin Bet office in Netanya. Fortunately, he was already at work. "Meyer, listen and don't ask questions," I instructed. "Shimon is badly wounded and in a Red Crescent ambulance coming from Tulkarim. We also have a wanted terrorist detained in the vehicle. We need you to call the border police guardhouse outside Tulkarim and tell them to let us through without hold-ups. Also, contact Laniado Hospital and tell them we will be at their casualty entrance in twenty minutes. They must admit Shimon at once – no paperwork. He will need a massive blood transfusion. His blood is the same as mine, type O. It would also help if we had a police escort part of the way," I said, before concluding: "Meet us at Laniado."

Thank God for quick thinkers. Asking no questions, Meyer replied, "*Beseder*!* See you there!"

"Drive to the guardhouse," I told the terrified driver. Seconds later, we were there. I could hear the phone ringing as we pulled up. The officer who answered it nodded, looked up at us, and waved the ambulance through.

"Get out!" I barked at the driver, banging on the divide between the cab and the back, and yelling for Gadir to release the medic on his side. I shouted out of the window to the officer manning the guardhouse: "Let them go back to Tulkarim! They've been a great help to us!"

Taking over the driver's seat, I sped off down the main road to Netanya with the siren screaming, breaking every speed limit and overtaking on the wrong side of the two-track road.

"Faster! faster!'" Gadir shouted from the back, "Shimon is fading! I cannot keep him alive much longer!"

The police escort met us several kilometres down the road at the Beit Lid junction, and, adding their siren to ours, got us to Laniado Hospital in a record 10 minutes. The emergency room staff were waiting for us, and I saw a deathly pale Shimon wheeled into a curtained cubicle. Meyer Jephet was also waiting, and as soon as Shimon had been admitted, he turned to me.

"I'll give you a little longer, but not much more. It's obvious that the three of you have got yourselves deep in the shit, and I don't want any of it to rub off on me," he said brusquely. "Clearly, Shimon is very badly wounded, and I only hope that he survives. The doctors were not optimistic. As soon as we know

* *Hebrew: OK; all is well.*

more, I want the full story from you, Dani. Not your usual bull, there is obviously more going on than I know about. I went way over the boundary for you, and I want to hear the real, unedited version!"

I fully understood Meyer's position. "Meyer, I hate to say this, but you are 100 percent right. My very deepest thanks; I know you went way out on a limb for us. Gadi and I can never repay you for your help, and if – please God – Shimon pulls through, he will agree with all his heart. I'd tell you the full story now but I don't think I'll be able to speak coherently until we hear how Shimon is doing and get some treatment for our own wounds." As I spoke, I nursed my mauled hands, which were beginning to sting now that the adrenaline of the morning was wearing off.

Meyer's icy blue eyes stared into mine, seeming to pierce right through me. "Right. Like I said, I'll give you a little longer. Shimon is also my close friend and comrade. But when the time comes to talk, it will be your head on the block, Dani. I know Gadir from way back, and anything he might have done will only be because you sweet-talked him into it. I have to give some sort of report to headquarters, and I'll promise them the full, true and unedited version today – and today means today, not tomorrow. Now go and wait for news on Shimon. Call me on my cell as soon as he is out of theatre."

So saying, Meyer strode briskly out of the room, leaving us to worry not only about Shimon, but also about the really deep hole we had dug ourselves into. "Gadi, I'm truly sorry about what I've got you involved in," I said, "I promise I'll make it right somehow!"

Gadir was less than convinced by the rather patronizing view Meyer took of him as an unassuming Bedouin tracker. "Dani," he replied, "I am a grown man. You did not talk me into anything – to tell the truth, I enjoyed most of it. I had thought that my fighting days were way behind me. Now I feel at least 10 years younger. I should really get myself back into training."

He was articulating exactly my own feelings, but for now my mood remained grim. I flung one arm over his shoulder, hugging him to me for a second before grimacing from the pain in my throbbing wrist. With that, we left to wait for news of Shimon.

Chapter 12

Word on Shimon was long in coming. We were still in the waiting room an hour later, when Meyer returned to say it was now or never. He needed our story in order to get the investigation moving forward.

"Right, Dani," said Meyer curtly, "I know I said I'd wait until Shimon was out of the operating theatre, but the top brass have come down on me, and I need some answers now. As you know, I've broken a lot of rules to get you here and have Shimon admitted with no questions asked. Now I want to hear the whole story, without your usual editing, and it had better be good – there has been enough of a *balagan** already, with you three sneaking off on a completely unauthorised mission to Tulkarim of all places! How I am going to cover up for you lot and complete all the paperwork I really don't know!"

"Calm down, Meyer," I said confidently, "when you hear what it's all about, you'll be only too happy to have been involved. Most likely there'll be a medal and a promotion for you when you follow up on all this. We'll have to leave it to you from here on in; we have no real authority to go forward with it."

"No real authority? You have no authority at all!" Meyer exploded. Checking himself, he went on in a measured voice: "As for medals, I have enough already, useless as secret service medals are. If it's true you haven't got me into shit, I'll settle for a good steak and chips at Pundak ha Yam – with you paying the bill. Now, no more of your sweet talk and bullshit, I want the whole story, and I want it now!"

"Right, Meyer, you certainly deserve it." With no further ado, I gave him a concise and virtually unedited account of what we had

---

* Hebrew: *Complete and utter mess-up.*

done since Gadir went undercover at the Surf Crest Hotel. I informed him of how we had traced Jibril to Tulkarim, ending with the story of how we managed to bring him back with us in the back of the ambulance. I neglected to tell him that we had left two dead bodies behind in the basement of the Tulkarim house – there was simply no way I could unload that on him on top of everything else. I was pretty sure that Jibril's group would keep it quiet for the sake of their men's morale. They'd probably just put it down to a 'work accident.' And Meyer would have more than enough problems returning the Red Crescent ambulance. I amused myself with the thought that he could swap it for one or two of the many cars stolen every day in Netanya, and smuggled to Tulkarim chop shops.

"If you guys are right about tactical nukes, then everything you've done is justified – although I'm still not thrilled about the mess you've left for me to clean up," Meyer said when I was finished. "For now, you and Gadir had better get your own wounds treated. Shimon will be in the intensive care unit for some time, and I must tell you that they are not holding out a lot of hope for him."

"As for our friend Jibril, I will see that he is taken undercover to Shabak headquarters and thoroughly interrogated. We'll soon shake the truth out of him. If I can – and only if I get the OK from above – I'll keep you in the picture. But only – and hear me well – on one condition! That you two promise not to run off on any more unauthorised missions. Now get yourselves off to casualty, I will see that they don't ask too many questions. We'll be in touch later on so you can help me out with the paperwork.

"By the way, how did all three of you get so badly wounded bringing in one suspect? A bit past it now, are we?" he winked, "Or were there other casualties that I don't know about?"

I put my hand to my head. "Neither of us are at our best, Meyer," I said, looking over at a worse-for-wear Gadir. Lets talk later. I promise you that steak at Pundak ha Yam. One last word though – I have a hunch that Mario is somehow involved in all this. It might be a good idea to ask him a few gentle questions."

Gadir and I made our way to the casualty department, leaving Meyer with the admin headache we had unloaded on him.

Laniado is the only hospital in Netanya, serving a population of some 200,000 residents of the city, as well as numerous *moshavim* and *kibbutzim** on the periphery. Run by a religious organisation, staffed by devout medical personnel, and financed solely by donations, it had the distinction of being the only hospital in Israel never to go on strike. Shimon would be well looked after here, and the doctors and nurses would give him a quality of care and loving attention that would not be available at some of the more advanced and better equipped hospitals, such as Tel ha Shomer in Tel Aviv, which treated seriously injured soldiers on a regular basis.

Still, as Shimon himself would surely have said to us, "*Zeh ma she yash*," – that's all that there is! We had no other option. On an unofficial and unauthorised mission, there was no way we could have called in a helicopter to ferry him to Tel ha Shomer.

The nurses in the casualty department, accustomed to treating road accident victims and minor household injuries, made a few puzzled comments about our multiplicity of wounds, but true to Meyer's assurances asked no questions other than the strictly medical ones. After our stab wounds had been cleaned and bound up, we were wheeled off for head x-rays.

As usual, Gadir found fun in the situation. "If these religious ladies could read all your wicked thoughts from the x-rays, you would soon be out on the street, Dani," he chuckled.

"Nonsense!" I quipped. "They would most likely find it very interesting and a welcome change."

Nearly two hours later, with our wounds cleaned and dressed and our head wounds deemed minor by the x-rays, we were told to relax and lie down to ensure there was no concussion from our respective blows to the head. Promising to obey doctors' orders, we immediately reneged and sneaked out to wait outside the intensive care unit to get news on Shimon.

Suddenly, I remembered Shimon's current lady friend, Adinah. He would want me to get in touch with her – he was seriously wounded and it seemed only right that she should be in the picture.

Returning to the reception area, I found an unoccupied

* Hebrew: *Communal settlement.*

public phone, but as usual no phone book. I knew that she managed a sex shop in central Netanya, but could not for the life of me remember the name – no way that the religious staff could help me there.

I went outside and got into a waiting taxi. Remembering only that the shop was located in an alley near Bank Mizrahi, I asked the driver to get there fast. Ten minutes later, we pulled up outside the bank.

After paying the taxi driver, I walked around the neighbourhood and soon found the shop. It was perfectly located: central enough to be easily available to its customers but positioned discreetly enough not to offend the sensibilities of the religious community. At the same time, it provided an equally discreet entrance and exit for shoppers wanting to keep a low profile.

As I walked in, I was immediately greeted with a warm hug from Adinah. "Hi, Dani! What brings you here? Shopping for adult entertainment?" she said with a laugh in her eyes, knowing there was no way I was a customer.

For the face of a sex shop, Adinah was a suitably voluptuous young lady, with a smooth olive complexion and pitch-black hair. Her slightly guttural accent gave away her Moroccan family background.

I smiled at the joke she had made at my expense. "Hi Adinah. Just visiting, not buying. I came to let you know that Shimon has been involved in an accident. He's in Laniado Hospital; they're operating on him as we speak."

Her eyes widened, and her mouth opened to emit a barely audible gasp. "I knew that something must be wrong!" she blurted. "He promised me a night out at the cultural centre to see that new play. When he never came or phoned, I simply could not understand it. But Dani, what can I do? I can't just close the shop – the owner will kill me."

"Adinah, love," I reassured her, putting my hand on her shoulder to anchor her. "Shimon is in good hands at Laniado, and there's nothing we can do until the doctors are finished with him. I promise that as soon as there is news I will call you. Just give me a business card so I can contact you here, and jot down your cellphone number just in case."

"My cellphone is dead; I forgot to charge it," she muttered, her mind clearly focused on the thought of Shimon in a hospital bed, out of reach.

"Do you have a home number I can call you on if it's after working hours?" I asked. "You won't be able to call me at Laniado; in an hour or two all cell calls will be barred for Friday evening – it violates *Shabat*.*"

"Sorry Dani, they cut off my landline," she said, her eyes meeting mine suddenly, as if she had been brought back from a far distance. "I forgot to pay the bill."

Well, that was Adinah all over – a lovely lady, great figure, and as warm hearted and caring as anyone I knew. Simply a little scatterbrained. She and Shimon had been an item for the last six months, and we had often double dated with my girlfriends of the moment. Unlike Shimon, I had not managed any long-term relationships since my last divorce. In fact, I had seen more of Adinah than any other woman since my last marriage ended. No wonder I sometimes caught myself competing with Shimon for her favour.

"Right. Well, as soon as I have news I'll get in touch with you somehow. Now I must get back to Laniado in case there's been any progress with Shimon."

Before I left, she gave me a hug, squeezing a bit tighter than usual, as if doing so might give Shimon a better chance. Then I turned around and left the shop – without ever really having gone inside. We had spoken just inside the doorway the entire time.

I hailed a passing taxi, and we sped back to Laniado. There, I was greeted with the news that Shimon had been placed in an artificially induced coma. Gadi put me in the picture.

"They say it will give his brain a chance to rest while the medical support systems keep him going," he reported, "it should give him a better chance to heal."

"How long do they say this will take?"

"They spoke of a 24-hour period. Nothing will happen until Sunday or Monday."

At that moment, a sweet young nurse, Sarah – who was probably dodging conscription through community service – came into

---

* *Hebrew: Sabbath.*

the waiting room. We had got acquainted during the x-rays earlier in the day.

"You have heard the news, Dani," she said. "There is really nothing you can do here. Both of you are suffering from wound trauma of your own. Just go home, rest, and we will be in touch. I have both of your cellphone numbers."

Gadi and I looked at each other, uncertain whether we could bring ourselves to leave Shimon alone here after he had almost died trying to save us. Eventually, I shrugged in defeat. "I expect she's right," I said, "you go and see your family, Gadi, and I'll be off home. I'll send a text message to Adinah." Hopefully she would pick the message up this evening when she recharged her phone.

Having felt years younger at the start of the day, Gadir was wearing his true age once again as we parted ways for the evening. He looked the way I felt as he exited the hospital: strength sapped; shoulders slumped.

.

Chapter 13

I went home, had a hot shower and phoned Adinah. She must have recharged her cellphone in anticipation of news from the hospital: she answered immediately.

"Hi Dani, what news?"

"I'm just back from the hospital," I responded, "they've put Shimon under deep sedation, and won't bring him out until Sunday."

"Well, at least that should help him recover," she said. "Is there anything else I should know?"

"Not really," I replied, feeling tired and ready for sleep. But suddenly I thought about poor Adinah counting away the uncertain hours as Shimon awaited his fate. "Since we have time to kill," I suggested, "Let's get together tomorrow and try to take our minds off it. Why not meet me at that new beach café on the Sironit beach? I'll tell you everything I can about what happened."

"OK," she said – Sironit was a beach where we had all spent many happy weekends. "What time is good for you?"

I thought for a moment. "Let's say 11h30. In time for lunch."

That settled, I collapsed onto my bed. The hot shower must have relaxed me – I fell into a sleep that felt as deep as Shimon's.

I awoke the next morning with sunlight streaming into the room – I had forgotten to close the curtains. Just as well, or I might have overslept. It was a beautiful day: the sun bright in the sky and the birds singing away as if all was well with the world. I looked at my watch. There was still time to drive to Laniado and check on Shimon.

When I arrived, there was a new head nurse on duty in the ward. I reintroduced myself.

"Yes," she said, introducing herself as Vera, "I know about you. Your friend is still in an induced coma, helping him to recover from the trauma he has suffered. Nothing further is likely to happen today, but give me your cell number and, if there is any news this evening, I'll call you."

It was disappointing to know there was nothing I could do for my friend but wait while the life support systems kept him going. I phoned Gadi to put him in the picture, and then left for the beach.

The café was almost full, but I knew the owner, and he put a little table out for me, right in front, almost on the water's edge. I looked at my watch: it was nearly 11.30. Yet I waited and waited, wondering if Adinah had thought better of our lunch date. I realised I was really looking forward to seeing her again. Perhaps it would be better if she didn't arrive. She was Shimon's girl after all, even if somewhere inside me I wished differently.

While I was musing, a shadow fell over the table. Startled, I looked up, and there stood Adinah. As was her custom, she wore a mini that showed off her long, shapely legs. She was sporting a cleavage that enhanced her natural assets. Inwardly, I blushed at this inappropriate attention to her appearance, but she really looked lovely. Her natural olive complexion glowed with a touch of rosy makeup. Her lipstick was a deep red, and there was a smile in her almond-shaped eyes.

What a sight! I could hardly be blamed for noticing.

I stumbled up and pulled out a chair for her. "So great to see you, Adinah! You look really lovely," I said in all honesty.

"Thanks," she said. "And what a beautiful day you have for us, Dani! And a table right on the sea! You must have *proteksia** here." She always found something to smile about. Maybe that was the source of her appeal – that infectious optimism and zest for life.

"Yes, the guy who owns this place is an old mate," I admitted. "Now, what would you like to eat and drink?"

We chose a meal of pita, humus, tehina and falafel balls,

---

* *Hebrew: Personal influence.*

with a mix of salads: sliced cucumber, a tabbouleh of chopped tomatoes, onions and cucumbers, and pickled beetroot. Served alongside this was a spicy Turkish dip, olives – both black and green – a potato salad and a large plate of crisp french fries. Adinah asked for a fresh orange juice, while I had my regular Goldstar beer.

We spoke little until the food and drink arrived. We fumbled for a connection through the minutes of halting smalltalk, uneasy being alone in each other's company for the first time. We were both very aware of Shimon's absence, and its cause.

When the waitress brought our meal, there was hardly room for it all on the small table. "*Beteavon,**" I said, and we clinked our glasses together and tucked in.

Simple, but very satisfying, the food made me think of Shimon in his unconscious state at the hospital. In spite of myself, I felt grateful to be alive; glad that I was here, under the clear sky, with a breeze on my face and a beautiful woman, full of life, at my side.

The food, sun and sea made for a great ambiance, and we soon found ourselves talking quite naturally. We spoke of Shimon, and our times together. We reminisced about our respective schooldays, and I told Adinah a few sanitised stories of my army service. Like most Israeli girls, she too had been in the army, and had more than a few tales of her own to tell.

The day wore on and we could not stop talking. Finally, a moment's silence fell over the table and I felt suddenly self-conscious again, enjoying Adinah's company while Shimon lay senseless on a hospital bed.

I looked away, and when our eyes met again, she gazed at me intently. "Dani, I really like you," she reflected, her brown eyes open, "we seem to have so much in common." She was voicing was both of us were feeling, but I knew it could go no further.

"Me too, Adinah," I said, cutting her line of thinking short, "but we also have Shimon in common. Please God, he will recover and we will continue to be friends as we are now."

By now, the sun was setting, and we watched its fiery red core disappear slowly behind the horizon, almost as if it was

---

* *Hebrew: Bon appetit.*

sinking into the sea.

"Sorry, Dani," Adinah said, collecting herself as if to leave, "I'm afraid I have to go now – the boss wants me to open up on Saturday nights."

"*L'hitraot,** Adinah, its been great spending the day with you. I'll keep in touch – let you know how Shimon is progressing."

Before turning her back to depart, she met my eye one more time: "I'll be at the shop tomorrow morning if you have any news," she said, "and please, Dani, I hope I'll see you soon."

Back at Laniado, I was to be told to be patient – there really would not be any news until Sunday. I stopped to look in on Shimon, who was still on life support. His face had not brightened at all from yesterday's deathly pallor, and for a few minutes I watched the bleeping monitors, expecting a crisis at any moment. None came; the machines continued to live for my friend.

I went home, phoned Gadi, watched the news for a few minutes, and went to bed. It was hard to sleep; my mind was a jumble of images, of Shimon and his desperate fight, and of Adinah and our day together. Eventually I resorted to another of my expired sleeping pills and fell into a sweaty sleep, one image chasing the other in my dreams.

The next day, I woke up early, my mind still muddled from the sedative. I dressed and headed back on the now regular track to Laniado – luckily less than two kilometres away from my house.

Gadi was there before me, looking glum. "No news," he reported. I sat and waited with him on the plastic chairs. Nurses and doctors passed in and out of the intensive care ward, their faces forbidding, ignoring us completely. Two hours later, there was still no word.

"To hell with this Gadi," I said, "I'm going inside. Worst case scenario, they'll just throw me out." Another nurse exited the ward and walked straight past, the steel doors swinging slowly closed behind her. Before they closed completely, I was up and dodging my way through.

* *Hebrew: Farewell.*

There were five beds in a row, each within a curtained cubicle. Most had the curtains partly opened in front, revealing patients hooked up to computer monitors with endless tubes and and wires connected to their bodies.

All the monitors beeped and green graph lines oscillated up and down the screens. All except one, that is. Shimon's monitor was ominously silent; the graph a lifeless horizontal line.

Green gowned doctors and nurses were huddled around the bed, doing nothing. As I reached his bed and saw his muscular body lying motionless and inert, I heard a doctor say, "It's no use Sarah, we've lost him."

The words came out of my mouth of their own accord. "No! No!" I yelled blindly. "You can't give up, he's strong; he'll make it! Do something! There must be something more you can do. Electric shock – mouth-to-mouth – something, anything!"

I was screaming like a madman.

They all turned to me, startled by my sudden appearance, and a doctor demanded to know who I was and what I was doing there.

"Dani Mafouz!" I shouted back. "I came here with Shimon two days ago, he's my friend. My blood brother!" I blurted, staring at his wrecked torso. "He got his wounds saving my life. You cannot let him die!" It was unthinkable. Shimon had been wounded countless times; seen countless hospital beds, and always recovered. "Don't just stand there!" I screamed, "Help him!"

A nurse made her way to my side. It was the gentle Sarah whom we had met on Friday. She gently took my hands in hers, and looked me straight in the face. "Dani, we have done everything humanly possible. We never give up." Looking into her earnest face, I knew it was true. "Human life is sacred to us – no matter who the patient is. We have fought to save Shimon for hours, and there was nothing more that we could do for him. Please believe me."

As Sarah's brown eyes filled with tears, I knew that Shimon was dead. He would never again laugh and joke with me. Looking at the body that was no longer Shimon, I felt an enormous void inside, as if everything within me had suddenly been emptied out.

Slowly I turned and went to break the news to Gadir. Shimon had completed his last mission at the cost of his own life.

Chapter 14

Gadir and I sat side by side on the plastic hospital chairs, staring at the floor as a cleaner with a mop made his way around our feet. Shimon was gone, and the mission he had died for was now out of our hands.

At least Gadir had a family to go home to. Me: a big, empty house and a clear schedule until the next training session – and even that meant little with both Shimon and Gidon gone for good. We quickly filled the yawning silence with a discussion about how to go forward: notifying loved ones and ex-army pals; making funeral arrangements.

I took it upon myself to contact Shimon's family, such as it was. His parents were both dead, leaving only the brother and sister he hadn't visited since before his last divorce.

Both were genuinely grieved despite the lapse in contact over the past few years, and offered to take care of all the formalities, perhaps as some form of atonement. With the funeral commandeered by Shimon's brother and the venue and catering for the family's seven days of mourning provided by his sister, I was left with little to do. Just a few more calls to make: two ex-wives who would probably miss the alimony more than Shimon himself, and Adinah.

Adinah. How could I break the news to her – especially after we had spent the last day of Shimon's life enjoying ourselves at the beach? Certainly I couldn't do it over the phone. I didn't want to break the news to her at work, but there seemed little option. Although it was one of Israel's larger towns, Netanya was still a village at heart, and news of Shimon's death would spread like wildfire through the local grapevine. I couldn't let Adinah hear the news from some barely familiar acquaintance or customer, so I drove to the shop as soon as I had informed the family.

I had to knock on the shop door when I arrived; it seemed Adinah was just catching up with paperwork. I sighed with silent relief when I realised that the shop was not open and that our conversation would not be overheard by shoppers browsing for porn or creatively coloured vibrators.

Adinah unlocked for me. One look at my face told her the devastating news. "Dani! Shimon's worse than we thought?"

Our eyes met silently for a long moment. I swallowed, trying to dislodge the unspeakable words. I cleared my throat and spoke. "He died, Adinah. As I got there, he died. There was nothing more they could do to save him," I looked away, trying to spare her my own emotions, "He sacrificed himself for us... and I didn't even get to say goodbye."

As I spoke, Adinah's vibrant face gradually froze into a mask of disbelief. She looked at me pleadingly, as if waiting to hear that it was all a bad joke. But all I could do was stare back in silence. After an excruciating minute I gathered the courage to reach out for her shoulder, trying to steady her as she tried without success to make sense of Shimon's death. At my touch, her face crumpled and her shoulders slumped.

"Dani! Tell me it isn't so!" She clutched at my arms, tears now streaming out of her eyes. "It can't be! Please, Dani, tell me it's not true!"

I couldn't think of anything adequate to say. "I'm sorry Adinah. We have lost our greatest friend."

Adinah was sobbing uncontrollably, and shaking her head blindly. "Let me take you home," I said, trying to make myself useful, "you can't work in this state. Not on a day like this." She didn't resist, and with some mute gestures and sniffed instructions, Adinah guided me through the motions of locking up the shop.

Adinah lived in a quiet neighbourhood only a short way from the bustling city centre. The peaceful tree-shaded street seemed light years away from the coldly clinical hospital and the horrors of Tulkarim. I walked her to the door, carrying her files, but she fumbled and dropped her keys when we got there. Her hands were shaking and she seemed ready to collapse. I had no choice but to take the keys and help her inside the dark, shuttered apartment.

We crossed the threshld like Siamese twins, joined at the hip. Adinah's right arm was clutched around my waist for support, with my left arm hooked under her right shoulder, propping her up. As I twisted awkwardly backward to close the door without letting the files slip from under my right arm, I found my left hand cupping Adinah's breast. Dropping the files in my embarrassment, I freed my hand from under her arm, blushing furiously.

Seemingly oblivious to my garbled apology, Adinah turned her and enclosed me with her other arm, her tear-streaked face resting damply on my chest. As I tried gently to prise myself out of her embrace, she stepped back suddenly, a look of confusion and hurt on her face. She stood there looking helpless, her tight dress clumsily hitched and her eyelids smudged with wet mascara.

I had never seen smooth, perfect Adinah look anything other than stylish and sexy. But right then, seeing her disheveled for the first time, with her face damp and blotchy and a bra strap peeking unselfconsciously out from under the lycra of her dress, I felt an enormous depth of empathy for her: lost and abandoned by her lover. I also felt suddenly aroused, in spite of my embarrassment.

I reached my hands out to cup her wet face. Wiping a tear away with my thumb, I bent and kissed her closed eyes. She lifted her face up to meet my lips and kissed me hungrily. As her mouth met mine, all my good intentions – to respect what had been Shimon's; not to take advantage of Adinah's vulnerability – simply disappeared.

Briefly, the old truism laughingly cited by army buddies in younger days flashed through my mind: "a standing cock has no conscience." But I knew that my need to fill the emptiness Shimon had left behind was just as strong as Adinah's. The more I felt her need, the more I myself was aroused, and in a mad frenzy I found myself violently unzipping her dress and forcing it from her shoulders as her hands clasped my jaw, pressing her open mouth into my own. Her bra soon followed the rest of her clothes to the floor, freeing her large, firm breasts. As I felt their weight in my hands and her nipples hard against my fingers, Adinah uttered a low gasp and began fumbling wildly with my belt and jeans. I stepped out of them without letting go of her.

Locked together, we moved across the floor, my shirt falling behind us before we tumbled awkwardly onto the nearest couch. For so long I had secretly longed to see Adinah unclothed, but now that we were naked together we were clutching each other so tightly that I could only feel her body and hardly see it at all.

Unfortunately, it seemed that she could see mine. She caressed my recent bruises and fingered the scars on my chest and stomach. I knew that I was not the fit young paratrooper that I had once been, and hoped that my visible extra weight would not repel her. But she seemed more concerned with the damage war had inflicted on me. "Dani," she whispered, "where did you get all these scars?" There was no way I wanted to enter into a discussion about my scarred body and scabbed wrists, but her touch was gentle and loving, and as she rubbed her nakedness against me, I was in no position to resist. Fingering the scar under my right nipple as she sucked it, she persisted.

"Dani, that's a really big scar; did you have an operation there?"

Struggling to put the sentence together, I responded: "It's a souvenir from the battle of Karameh; some of the other marks as well. I got a bit shot up there." And then, "Please Adinah, no more questions," as I forced a hand between our sweating bodies to caress the hard nub of excitement between her legs. As my fingers entered her I felt wetness pouring from her – warm, wet and wonderful.

It was more than I could bear, and my own throbbing erection demanded its turn. As I entered her and slid easily inside, her hands gripped my back fiercely: I could feel her fingernails leaving tracks on my skin. I could think of nothing more than the moment.

When I felt myself coming, I slid down her sweaty body to prolong our escape. As I probed inside her and rolled my tongue against the tight bud of her clitoris, she went completely berserk, bucking up and down against my face and gasping as she became wetter and wetter.

I too could no longer restrain myself: my cock felt swollen to twice its size. Rolling over onto my back I gripped Adinah by the waist and lifted her on top of me, where we were reunited: her streaming wet centre embracing my pulsing erection.

I felt that we were no longer two separate people. She rode me urgently, pressing downwards onto my straining hips. Faster and faster we moved together, until there was nothing left but to surrender to the climax.

Adinah lay at my side, her left hand clutching my right, our fingers linked together. Light filtered through the slats of the dimly lit room, and I saw dust motes riding the sunbeams. I noticed yesterday's dress flung over the back of a chair, and the coffee table cluttered with abandoned coffee cups.

In the wake of our passion I felt suddenly guilty again. This was Shimon's girlfriend beside me – lover of the friend who had died to save me; who was not yet even buried. As I opened my mouth to speak, uncertain what to say, but compelled to somehow apologise, I felt Adinah's finger sealing my lips. I met her eyes, and she simply shook her head. Both of us knew that words could not bring Shimon back or undo what we had done to forget.

I encircled Adinah with one arm, and she leaned in to me, resting a hand on my chest. We fell asleep right there, on the floor, thoughts of Shimon's untimely death momentarily banished.

Chapter 15

On the day of the funeral, the skies were heavy with the threat of rain – usually so welcome in Israel. The potholed drive through the city's old industrial area to the cemetery only worsened my depressed mood. Every rain-filled rut splashed dirty water onto the windshield, and the combined effort of the rain and the wipers seemed only to smear a mud-brown filter over the glass, almost completely obscuring the view.

As a result, I took a wrong turn on the winding road and got lost in an area I had never seen before, where I could find no-one to correct my bearings. When I finally arrived at the cemetery, sweating from anxiety, and looking disrespectfully rumpled, the mourners were already standing around the open bier with Shimon's body wrapped in his talit prayer shawl. Everyone was waiting for me to deliver the eulogy.

Another wave of gloom descended on me as I hurried towards the subdued group. Shimon had given his life for us, and this was how I repaid him. As if it wasn't bad enough that I had found comfort in his lover's arms, I was now arriving late and dishevelled to pay my last respects. Inwardly, I sent up a heartfelt apology to my friend, and swore to him that no matter what happened to me or how long it took, his death would be avenged.

"We all knew and loved Shimon, and we are here today to mourn his untimely death," I began after gathering my strength. "He died as he had lived: a brave soldier fighting for his country to the last. He did not die in uniform or on an official mission, so he is being buried here as a civilian, rather than in the military cemetery amongst his fallen comrades. Sadly, there has been no military guard of honour to accompany him to his grave; he has not received the ceremony that was his due.

"But that would not have mattered to Shimon. He was always a man of the people, happiest sitting with his friends at a café table and talking on every subject under the sun, from soccer, to world affairs, to the state of the nation. Shimon always had a new joke, a new story, and a helping hand to offer to any of his friends in trouble.

"For security reasons, I cannot share the details of Shimon's last mission, but suffice it to say that he died at the hands of terrorists in an unauthorised and virtually solo mission to track down a very dangerous gang of criminals. In saving both the mission and the lives of his fellow agents" – I cleared my throat – "he lost his own life.

"We will all remember you, Shimon! Your smile, your courage in adversity, and your unselfishness – which ended in the final sacrifice of your own life for others! Goodbye, my friend."

As I looked up, my duty done, I caught sight of Adinah, eyes downcast, hands cupping her face as if in prayer. None of Shimon's ex-wives had deigned to come, and the remaining members of his family stood reserved and formal, but unemotional. Shimon had not been in close contact with any of them; even his siblings had not seen him in the past five years or so. Gadi and I had shed our tears at the hospital and stood dry-eyed at the cemetery, my own guilty feelings weighing me down.

The religious formalities went smoothly enough. After the last spadefuls of earth had been thrown, and stones of remembrance placed by those closest to Shimon, the assembly quickly dispersed. Everyone wanted to get out of the wind and rain, and back to the warmth of their homes and workplaces. Adinah left separately, as she had come. Out of respect, we said little to each other at the funeral, although our eyes met several times, with a silent acknowledgement that we would see each other again.

Soon, only Gadir and I were left, trudging slowly up the slight hill to the cemetry gates. "Gadir, we must talk," I said, thinking of my pledge to avenge our friend. We agreed to rendezvous at my place in half an hour's time.

Gadir drove away, leaving me alone with my thoughts on the drive back into town. Despite my silent oath to Shimon, I still had no idea how, where, and when any vengeance I had in mind would play out. The lonely drive home provided an opportunity to get my thoughts in order, but by the time I arrived home, and found Gadir already parked outside, I was still far from any concrete plan of action.

Opening the front door, with Gadir at my side, I suddenly froze. There was a distinct smell of cigarette smoke in the air. Putting my finger to my lips, I looked over at Gadi. Clearly, he had noticed the trace of smoke before me: he was already crouched in an attack position at the side of the doorway.

Slipping off our shoes, we moved silently into the house. As we entered the living room, I stole right while Gadi dodged left. The man lying back on the couch began to laugh at our stealth tactics. It was Meyer Jephet.

"What took you so long?" he asked, "I must have dropped off to sleep waiting for you."

"Meyer, you *mamzer*!* What are you doing in my house?" I exclaimed. "How did you get in? Don't you realise that you nearly gave me a heart attack?"

"You're going to need to work on those nerves, Dani," Meyer drawled, unperturbed by my flustered reaction. "I came by to speak privately with you, and found the spare key you leave under the doormat. It's urgent, and I'm glad Gadir is here with you, because what I have to say concerns him too. Now calm down, make us a nice cup of coffee – two sugars for me – and we can talk together without all Netanya listening in."

I was in no mood for jokes. My face must have reflected the temptation to simply kick Meyer out, because Gadir, who knew my disposition all too well, suddenly spoke up. "Dani, let us have coffee and listen to the man," he said quietly, "it must be important if he has time to come here and wait for you during these busy times. Let us listen. A wise man listens first and acts afterwards."

I took Gadi's advice and went into the kichen to make a pot of strong, black coffee, flavoured with *hel* to make the cardamom-infused beverage that Gadir preferred.

* *Hebrew: Bastard.*

Back in the sitting room, I sat down and took a deep breath: "OK, Meyer, we're listening."

Chapter 16

Meyer took a deep slurp of his coffee, nodded appreciatively, and looked long and hard at both of us. I could see that he had slept little in the past few days: his deep-set blue eyes were pink with fatigue, and seemed to have retreated even deeper into their sockets. The grey streaks in his tousled black hair seemed more prominent than usual, and his usually shaggy eyebrows seemed to have taken on a life of their own. Normally a trim and fit 1.85 metres, he seemed to have shrunk in size, and slouched exhaustedly on the sofa. Undoubtedly he could see from the expressions on our faces that we were shocked at his appearance, but we made no comment.

Taking another pull at the mug of coffee, and almost finishing it in the process, he began talking at last.

"You guys have been through a very tough time in the last few days, and I know how much Shimon's death has upset you. But I must tell you that his sacrifice and your hard work has brought us very valuable information.

"You know the drill, but nevertheless I must swear you to secrecy on what I am about to tell you. Under no circumstances can you reveal anything without an OK from the military censors."

Meyer reached into his briefcase and produced two brief documents. "If I am to continue, I am forced to ask you both to sign these," he said, sliding the confidentiality agreements towards us over the coffee table.

Once the formalities were over, he gave us his piercing stare and continued: "Your capture of Jibril has uncovered a terrorist organisation we had no knowledge of until now."

Gadir and I exchanged a worried glance. Already, Israel faced a triple threat – what more could there be? Hamas, the Palestinian terrorist-organisation-come-political-party, was one. Its charter declared *jihad* the only solution to the Palestinian question – a seductive argument for Palestinians disillusioned with the corrupt and ineffective Fatah government. Hamas was pretty much independent. Though it received financial and material assistance from Iran, it also raised its own funds under the guise of Islamic charities across the world, and had a distinct agenda of its own.

Then, there was the Islamic Jihad, a movement committed to the creation of an Islamic Palestinian state through a 'holy war'. It, too, received financial backing from Iran, as well as from Syria. But, of course, it was no longer the force it had once been. The Palestinian president, Mahmoud Abbas, and his Fatah security force, was much quicker to act against the group nowadays.

Finally, there was Hizbolla, the Shi'a militia in Lebanon that in the last decade had continuously attacked across the border of Israel and was still calling for its destruction. Primarily dependant on Iran, it had up until the present confined most of its activities to attacks from the Lebanese territory, taking little or no part in terrorist activities inside Israel proper.

Seeing our looks of disbelief, Meyer confirmed: "Yes. Your efforts seem to have unearthed a completely new threat to our security. What we shook out of Jibril is that an overall umbrella organisation is being formed, comprising anti-Israeli and anti-US terrorist gangs that owe no allegiance to any national government."

Again, this was a very serious development. It seemed that the renegade Al Qaeda group, responsible for the 9/11 tragedies as well as many attacks in East Africa and Indonesia, was providing funding from its base in Afghanistan, using Osama bin Laden's billions to draw comparatively small, independent terrorist groupings into an anti-Western alliance.

"Al Qaeda is now backed by the new government in Iran, which is headed by the mad Mullahs and President Mahmoud Ahmadinejad, who, as you know, has his eyes set on a world without America or Israel."

"And a history without the holocaust or 9/11," I added, citing Ahmadinejad's well-known denials.

Meyer continued without pause: "On top of this new development, Iran's atomic energy programme is now only a matter of months from the capacity to produce at least a few atomic weapons – it seems the UN has run out of ideas to end the standoff on its uranium-enrichment activities. Obviously this is a problem considering Iran's anti-Zionist and anti-American rhetoric, but all that talk of America, 'the great Satan,' that whips up the support of the Islamic masses, obscures the fact that – believe it or not – Al Qaeda is also working towards a coup in Saudi Arabia, which will allow them to gain control of the world's oil supplies."

Meyer paused while we absorbed this information. But there was more. He recounted how Iran and Al Qaeda had purportedly acquired a supply of tactical nuclear weapons from impoverished scientists in the former Soviet Union. This was probably wht Gidon's informer would have told him, if their meeting had taken place.

Meyer sighed and said flatly: "We have no idea how many tactical nukes we're dealing with, or where they're located. Bin Laden has bases in Sudan and Afghanistan, and we know that he has recently struck a deal with Iran – once against him, now his active ally. Our own best guess – and it's only a guess – is that the weapons have been moved through Iraq, because of its proximity to the Russian source. They may have been smuggled to Syria just before the American invasion of Iraq.

"What we do know, however, is the location of Iran's uranium enrichment plants, and that's where it may be possible to launch a pre-emptive strike. After all, the capacity they are developing far outweighs the threat of a small cache of salvaged tactical weapons."

Meyer looked drained. I went to make another pot of coffee while he caught his breath. When I came back with another three steaming mugs, we rearranged outselves on the couches and Meyer went on.

"We have still another major problem," he said. "We took your friend Mario into custody as you suggested, and the information that we managed to get out of him is just as alarming. Through his contacts in the Netanya police, he has managed to form a network of security personnel who serve as informers. Originally, they provided information to protect his gambling and prostitution interests, but since Jibril began providing him with protection, they have been cooperating both with the Bin Laden ring, and Hamas leader Khalid Mashaal, now a close Iranian ally.

As you can imagine, they are being paid huge amounts into foreign accounts to pass on information."

It beggared belief. The Netanya police had never been entirely bona fide, but their usual under-the-table protection dealings were small fry compared with this.

"Israel's own forces assisting its enemies? This cannot be," said Gadir, echoing my own sentiments.

"Unfortunately it is so, Gadir," said Meyer. "We have identified a few of the bad apples, and they are all under covert surveillance. It'll take time to wrap up the whole gang though, because they work within a cell system – no single individual knows all the others.

"Time, however," said Meyer, inhaling from a cigarette he had just lit, "is something we don't have to spare. Nuclear weapons in terrorist hands can only lead to a conflagration of the entire Middle East. As a trainer within Gidon's unit you know this even better than I do, Dani." He took a deep breath, drained the last dregs of his coffee, and looked grimly at us.

"God knows I hate to do this, particularly at this time, but I have no option at the moment. I have been officially instructed to recruit the two of you to help us destroy one of the Iranian nuclear sites. You will be tasked with marking out the exact coordinates of the entranceway, so that it can be destroyed without collateral damage."

"Why us, Meyer?" I asked, disbelieving. "We're talking about the nuclear plants, not the tactical weapons our own investigations uncovered. This is an external security issue – the Mossad's* jurisdiction, surely. And not only are we internal security, we're pretty much over the hill." I looked at Gadir for affirmation. "Don't get me wrong, Meyer, we're keen to help. We don't want Shimon's death to be in vain. But the truth is, we're not in top condition, we've never done an external security mission before, and our inexperience could be a major liability," I trailed off there, disheartened by this reality check after earlier my enthusiasm to avenge Shimon's death.

"First," Meyer responded, "We know you're not spring chickens, but you've both had full training in Gidon's unit. You

---

Israel's external security and intelligence agency, much like the CIA.

may not be fit, but you're capable and trustworthy. Fitness we can work on. Trust we can't. There's no time to groom other agents.

"Second, the Mossad's experience is exactly their problem. Their agents have been in the field too long; if they were recognised in the wrong place at the wrong time, they could accelerate the threat rather than curbing it. So what we really need are unknowns operating under deep cover. Unfamiliar faces that won't raise any question marks."

He looked at us with a question in his eyes. Gadi and I looked at each other briefly, but we really had no need to talk. We had both sworn to avenge Shimon, and here we were being given an open ticket, with full government backing, to do just that. It was a rare opportunity for two middle-aged war-horses like us to return to action. We nodded affirmatively.

"Right," said Gadir, "but we reserve the right to approve the final plan of action and cover stories before we set out. We can accept danger, but there are limits." Both of us remembered the *fashlot** of certain previous operations, conceived by back-room heroes without discussion with the men at the sharp edge.

Meyer looked relieved. "Fair enough from my viewpoint, but you know I don't have the final say. I'll take it upstairs and come back to you tomorrow. If it's a go, you'll get an in-depth brief from the top.

"In the meantime, no discussion – even with your family, Gadir. We'll think up an acceptable story for them, and will see that they are well looked after in your absence. As for you, Dani, not a word to Adinah. Tell her that you have urgent family business in Germany. Not a word more!" I blushed violently. Apparently the Shabak really did know everything.

"We don't have much time," Meyer concluded, standing up. "Get your affairs in order and meet me in my office tomorrow. Gadir, drive me back to headquarters and we'll come up with a story for your family." With that, Meyer left, taking Gadir with him, and leaving me with my thoughts.

The more I contemplated the dual threats facing our nation – and indeed far beyond – the more convinced I became that the danger of the tactical nuclear weapons stash our work had so far

---

* *Hebrew: Blunder.*

uncovered was far outweighed by the danger from Iran, a wealthy, major power in its own right. While a tactical nuke could wipe out a small city, a regular nuclear bomb could destroy Israel – just as the Iranians had promised twice in recent weeks.

I had even less family left than Shimon had. No parents; no siblings. I really had nobody to worry about but Adinah. I hated the thought of lying to her, even for a good cause. And thoughts of her brought more thoughts of Shimon, renewing my determination to succeed in our proposed mission and to fulfil my promise of avenging his death.

I walked outside to breath in the sweetness of the rain-freshened air. Walking towards the sea, with the light fading and the horizon merging with the sea in a slate gray haze, I felt a deep sense of unity with my surroundings. As the waves crashed on the beach, and the last few birds soared and fluttered back to their evening hideaways, it seemed I was part of a heroic symphony. I found myself humming the opening chords of Beethoven's Fifth. Like all soldiers, I felt that if anything happened it would be to someone else, and I worried that I might have placed a family man like Gadir in mortal danger.

The sky darkened along with my thoughts, and I left the sea shore to find Adinah.

Chapter 17

The winter skies had cleared and the sun was doing its best to warm us up as Gadir and I met outside the suburban address Meyer had given us that morning. It was in Herzliya, a town midway between Netanya and Tel Aviv – about 20 minutes' drive.

I felt physically and emotionally drained after a long leave-taking with Adinah the previous night, and I could see that Gadir had also had problems explaining his sudden departure to his family. His normally happy, sunny face was set in a grave mask.

"Are you sure this is the right address, Dani?" Gadi asked. He was right, it looked like any suburban home.

"Only one way to find out. Lets go through the gate and ring the doorbell."

The door was opened by a young woman who looked enquiringly at us. "Do I know you?" she asked. "Er," I began, my brow furrowing with doubt, "I'm Dani, and he is Gadir. We are supposed to meet with Meyer Jephet here. Maybe we made a mistake in the address," I said.

"Come on in," she replied, closing the door firmly behind us. The small entrance hall looked normal enough. There was a child's bike leaning against one corner of the room, and a vase of flowers on the telephone table. She opened another door, and instead of the living room that I had expected to see there was a well-equipped office, complete with computers, fax machines, telephones and a plain-clothes security guard with a 9mm pistol holstered at his side. Another young man was carrying a Galil automatic rifle.

"Hand over your ID cards and stand where you are while we check you out for any concealed weapons," the woman instructed us. She checked our IDs on a nearby computer while the first guard frisked us.

"Sorry about that," she said once we were cleared, "but you can appreciate that we have to take all the usual precautions. Please follow me upstairs." So saying, she led us through another doorway, up a marble staircase and into another office, this one furnished only with a long table surrounded by government-issue office chairs.

Meyer was seated at one side of the table, and next to him was an elderly man who looked very familiar. The two of them rose to greet us as the anonymous young woman turned her back, closing the door behind her.

"*Shalom.** I am pleased that you agreed to help us," said the stranger, "my name is Moshe. First of all, let me condole with you on the deaths of your friends, Shimon and Gidon. I did not have the pleasure of knowing Shimon personally, but Gidon I knew well both as a friend and a colleague. They were good men, and will be missed by all who knew them." He resumed his seat and motioned for us to sit. "I would also like to congratulate the two of you on a job of work, however unusual and unofficial, well done. However, I am sure that you both realise that from now on there can be no more spur-of-the-moment decisions. It could cost us all dearly if there is no backup and chain of command."

"Moshe represents the highest levels of the organisation," Meyer interjected, seeing Gadi and I exchange a meaningful look. Neither of us were overly fond of strict procedures, and both had suffered unnecessary injuries in the field thanks to the best-laid plans of armchair heroes. Not least of these was the infamous botched operation at Karameh, where I had been lucky to come away with only an assortment of unsightly scars.

Moshe looked at us and laughed briefly, "I can see what the two of you are worrying about, just hear me out, then feel free to comment."

Before Moshe could say more, we had to sign another confidentiality agreement. That done, he proceeded to reveal more about the man we had captured in Tulkarim.

"Meyer has already explained why we are recruiting you,

---

* Hebrew: *Peace.*

but let me reiterate. You are the only people we know and trust who have had actual contact with the leading Hamas member, Jibril." Gadi and I listened intently, keen to know more about our man's true identity.

"Jibril is the right-hand man of Khaled Mashaal, who now heads up Hamas from his Syrian office. Mashaal is now virtually an official representative of Iran. All anti-Israeli policy is now directed by the Iranian Intelligence, with orders from the top level. It is carried out either through Hizbollah, in Lebanon, or Hamas in Syria and the Palestinian Authority areas.

"We know that Iran would like to wipe Israel off the face of the earth; their president has said as much," said Moshe, pausing to drink from a bottle of Mei Eden spring water, and to take a few deep breaths. His age was obviously telling on him, but his brain was as sharp as ever.

"Jibril is currently imprisoned, but we will organise a realistic escape. We will track him as far as we can, and then pass on the chase to you two, who will follow him to Iran. Any nuclear plans they are setting in place must be aborted at all costs, with a pre-emptive strike if absolutely necessary. We would prefer to avoid that and stay in the good books we've been in since our withdrawal from Gaza. Howevery, if we have no other option, so be it – the survival of our country and our people comes before flattering words from the international community."

Moshe moved to the wall behind him and lowered a roller-mounted map – one of many on the wall. This was a detailed map of Iraq, showing towns, villages and roads as well as the main cities. "I hope this will be clear to you," he said. "These maps are updated regularly and come to us courtesy of the CIA. Unbelievably, sanitised versions are even available on the Internet.

"Let's go over your cover stories before proceeding to the actual plan of action," said Moshe. "Dani, we know you are a second-generation Israeli. Your parents came here from Persia, and you spoke in Farsi and German before you spoke Hebrew. Your late father was German born, and as his son you, too, have a German passport. It was updated and reissued to you on a trip to Munich four years ago, and so has Munich as its place of issue."

Amazed that he knew so much about me, I could only nod in agreement. "Right, that takes care of that, then. German businessmen are always traveling to Iraq trying to sell reconstruction equipment. The German cover will explain your less than fluent Arabic.

"You, Gadir, are Bedu, and your tribe has close family connections with the Jordanian Bedouin loyal to the Royal Family," he began, facing my friend. Again I was amazed: as long as I had known Gadir, and as close as we were, I had not known this.

He too was virtually speechless. "That is so," he responded.

"We will be getting you a Jordanian passport," said Moshe, "we have already made all the necessary arrangements – not easy after the Mashaal affair, where our two 'Canadian' agents botched up an attempted assassination on him in Jordan.

"But in view of the atomic danger, and with a little help from our American colleagues, it will not be a problem. The passport will be suitably back-dated and border stamped, with previous visits to Iraq and Iran, coinciding with visits made by one of your namesakes, who is a wholesale merchant. The fact that your names are the same will give you extra cover."

Moshe looked from Gadir to me. "We will go over your covers in greater depth later, but in the meantime, please let me know if either of you see any basic problems. Let's take a coffee break while you think it through."

Gadir and I could see no immediate problem with the cover stories. As soon as we finished our coffee, Moshe stood up and went over to the wall map and began outlining the basic plan of action. I would go to Germany, and from there to the Jordanian capital of Amman, where I would meet up with Gadir. We would then travel by Land Rover to the Iraqi border, ostensibly with a commercial interest in the reconstruction efforts in that country. Jordan would be our best bet for a trouble-free entry into Iraq.

"To put you fully in the picture," said Moshe, "Iraq was never thoroughly searched by either the UN inspectors or American army teams. If they failed to find weapons at a specified site, the searchers never thought to turn over stones a few hundred meters away.

"Because of the UN weapons inspectors, Saddam moved tactical nuclear and chemical weapons from place to place in a continuous shell game. The bulk were airlifted to Syria just before the American invasion.

"As for the rest, we won't get bogged down in details that don't concern your mission. The bottom line is that we already have teams searching Iraq – that is one of the reasons why we are so thin in manpower resources. They will not be told about you two or your mission, only that there is another team – code name 'Shimon' – working in the area. Both teams will be given recognition codes if contact is necessary, but at this stage contact with our assets in Iraq or Iran will only be a last resort. We can't be sure whether or not they have been compromised thanks to our friend Mario. If – God forbid – you get into real trouble and are forced to make contact, they will respond immediately. But they will be at best a day's journey away – more once you enter Iran.

"For communication purposes, we have an agent located on a hilltop in Iraq, from which he can see into both countries using high-powered binoculars. You will report back via him where necessary. We don't want to break his cover, so contact him by the only the most secure possible means. A signaling lamp may be best."

Here, Moshe unrolled some more large, detailed maps from the wall, and, using a laser pointer, gave us our proposed route.

"The easiest entry point into Iraq is via the Jordanian/Iraqi border – not too difficult these days. You can then travel on a fairly good road to Ar Rutbah. From there, head south to Al Ramadi, and then on through some fairly rough country on the right bank of the Euphrates to An Nasiriya.

"You then follow the Euphrates until it joins the Tigris just north of the Basra area. Here you will be met by a good friend of ours: a high-ranking member of the British MI6. He is well known to the the local marsh Arabs, who have good cause to hate both the Iraqis and the Iranians. He will enlist their help to guide you through the marshes and across the Iraq/Iran border."

Moshe indicated a point on the map near the boundary between Iraq and Iran. "Assisted by the MI6 agent, you will travel through the marshes to a point near the border of Iran, not far from your destination," he said. "The main Iranian atomic plant is located deep underground near Natanz, which is midway between Kashan and Estahan, about 40 kilometres southeast of Kashan.

There is also a major reactor at Busheir – but we've already pinpointed its location. Now we need to do the same for the Natanz plant, and that is the crux of your mission.

"The Baluchi tribes of southeast Iran are smugglers (something like some of the Bedu, Gadir). As Sunni muslims, they oppose the majority Shiites controlling Iran, and provide a route to smuggle drugs from Afghanistan to Europe. In an emergency, they can be prevailed upon to help you, and to provide basic intelligence that will help you refine the target site.

"Our own information is that Jibril has been invited to inspect the Natanz site. This is to give the terrorist coalition encouragement to resume conventional attacks against Israel until all is ready for our proposed destruction.

"You have, in reality, two missions: to dispose of him – and no *fashlas** this time! – and to pinpoint the site precisely with satellite beacons that can be activated to guide our aircraft and missiles in when the final orders come for an attack. The beacons need to be placed at the entrance to the tunnel into the site – you can see them on our satellite images."

Moshe must have seen the looks of disbelief on our faces. "This is not some kind of wild dream," he said, soberly. "I'm sure you both realise that, however important and dangerous your proposed mission is, it is only one jigsaw piece in a complete and complex operation. We have just received information from our director of military intelligence that Iran has recently received 12 cruise missiles, with a range of 3,000 km, from a shipment that went astray from the Ukraine to Russia. Clearly, these could carry nuclear warheads.

"You most likely remember former generals Eitan Ben Eliyahu, once commander of our air force, and Yitzhak Ben-Israel, former head of military research and development, cautiously agreeing at a Netanya College symposium that Israel alone had both the will and the military capability to attack the Iranian nuclear sites.

"It was agreed that final planning for such an operation could be wrapped up in three months, and you will be pleased to

---

* *Hebrew: Bungles.*

hear that certain of the Emirate States have secretly given Israel and the United States the all-clear to over-fly their air-space. The CIA has been gathering information from Dutch AIVD agents on the ground in Iran for the last few years, with the aim of infiltrating and sabotaging its weapons industry. But with the upcoming elections in the US, I have my doubts if the incoming President will have the will or the power to join us in taking the final steps."

Meyer and Moshe went on to recount the equipment that would be made available to us, including concealed radiation meters that would help us identify the target, and any other equipment we deemed necessary. We would be fully trained in their use and briefed in more depth in the weeks to follow if we were to accept the mission.

There was no time to lose, so Gadi and I asked to speak privately while we thought the proposal through.

I knew that our mission was almost impossible based on the scant information available, but I also knew that there was little choice. This was our opportunity to avenge Shimon and Gidon – something I now saw we could never do on our own. In addition, I had in Gadi not only a close and dependable comrade, but also one of the world's best trackers, whose skills would be vital in the stony desert wastes. My German-Iranian background would also be invaluable in a tight corner.

"Look," I said to my friend, "this is a typical organisation scheme, asking just two of us to do the work of a whole platoon. Just getting to Natanz will be an enormous job – and it's only once we get there that we face the real danger!

"If the Natanz plant is buried deep underground, it will need exact pin pointing – even for a 'bunker-buster' bomb. We will have to get to the very heart of the complex – that's where the real danger lies, and Moshe knows it!" But my words belied the fact that I had no intention of refusing the mission.

Gadir thought for a moment or two, then nodded, "Natanz it is, and if by some miracle we survive, we will have made a priceless contribution to the survival of Israel."

We looked at each other, tense with anticipation, as we waited for Meyer and Moshe to return. In just a few moments, we would be giving our assent to the Natanz operation – a risk-fraught and almost impossible mission. Once we had collected a few belongings, we would return to the safe house and be out of touch with friends and family until we returned. If indeed we did return.

Chapter 18

Days of briefings and 10 weeks of training at Tzal'aim in the Negev desert followed. We heard things that we would never have believed possible, and returned to a level of fitness equally astonishing.

One briefing, by a leading expert on Iran, Yeshiyahu Hoshea, made a particularly strong impression.

"Hard as it may be to believe, Israel has a secret agent in the Iranian hierarchy," he said, after instructing us to call him Yeshi. "Believe it or not, his name is President Ahmadinejad."

Gadi and I looked at each other. "Is he insane?" Gadi mouthed to me. "Completely *meshuggah*," I whispered back.

Yeshi continued, with a grin. "Just listen, guys; I'll take questions afterwards." We leaned back and did as he asked – it certainly wasn't going to be boring.

He went on: "Thanks to his non-stop holocaust denial, Ahmadinejad has turned the US and Europe against Iran, and made us, the underdogs, remember the Six Day War once more.

"He has also succeeded in building a Sunni muslim camp, including the Gulf States and Saudi Arabia, into an anti-Iran coalition."

Yeshi took a sip of water from the glass on his table, and continued. "Because of his hardline policy, and denial of basic human rights, an Iranian opposition group has formed. They even have their own web-site: www.ncr-iran.org."

This was really surprising. Our ears pricked up even more.

"Did you know," Yeshi continued, "that nearly a year ago, an Iranian Falcon jet crashed in northwest Iran, with General Ahmed Kazemi, commander of the elite Revolutionary Guard forces, and another 12 high-ranking officers on board?

"A month later, an Iranian military transport plane crashed on take-off. On board: 30 high-ranking Iranian army officers. Shortly before that, a helicopter crash claimed the life of another high-ranking Revolutionary Guard officer."

Now we were really engrossed. Yeshi continued, "In all seriousness, however, Iran is determined, despite Western sanctions, to develop an atomic bomb. You will remember Ahmadinejad saying, during the Islamic summit conference in Malaysia, that only the complete destruction of Israel would ensure peace in the Middle East.

"Iran has no real air force, but has the Shihab missile, and new Ashoura intercontinental ballistic missiles, which you may know as ICBMs. Their range is over 2,000 km, putting not only Israel, but also northeastern America and all of Europe at risk.

"There are now over 3,000 centrifuges at work in the huge underground facility in Natanz, near the Iraq/Iran border. But Iran has spread its nuclear facilities across the territory. For instance, there is the site at Busheir, which is being openly supplied with enriched uranium by Russia. Russia claims that it exercises control over the supplies to Busheir, to ensure that the uranium cannot be used for atomic weapons. Natanz, therefore, poses the main danger to us, and is also the most difficult site to attack.

"A reinforced, electrified security fence surrounds this huge facility, built to hold over 5,000 centrifuges. Iran budgeted $1.4 billion for the plant's construction, in a country in which, despite huge oil revenues, many people are without work, and can barely feed themselves. The main hall is buried eight metres underground, and protected by successive layers of concrete slab, compressed earth, and other resistant materials."

Listening to this, we were getting really worried. "It doesn't take a genius to figure out that what they want us to do is virtually impossible," I whispered to Gadi. Yeshi pretended not to have heard.

"Normal bombs cannot penetrate Natanz; only the 'bunker-buster' bombs carried by B-2 Stealth bombers can do the job. President Bush recently authorised $88 million for the retrofit of B-2 bombers to carry bunker busters.

"Unfortunately, President Bush has limited time left in office, and it's unlikely his successor would dare to order an attack on Iran." Yeshi allowed his voice to rise for the first time. "Once more, Israel stands alone. It seems that our destiny, and indeed our very survival, rests once more only in our own hands."

In my hands and Gadi's, to be precise, I thought to myself. It was now clear that a do-or-die mission was being served up to us.

Although both of us had maintained a measure of physical fitness, the weeks that followed saw us through more and more grueling exercises to bring us up to peak condition. There was also a brief training course on survival, and what to do and say in the event of capture.

Weapons that we thought existed only in science fiction were revealed to us, and we were given free choice – the only limitation being what we could reasonably expect to carry in our Bergen backpacks.

A laser-guided mini anti-tank rocket was too good to pass up, however, and the launcher could be concealed as part of the roof rack on the Land Rover that would be driven by land to Jordan. Small satellite navigation aids could place us within metres of our position and could also serve as communication uplinks to our base. Plastic explosives were moulded to look like harmless mugs. Detonators were similar to spare spark plugs. The list went on.

My laptop computer – essential to any bright German businessman, could also serve a variety of purposes, including communication and missile guidance if needed. But despite all the hi-tech equipment on offer, I surprised everyone by insisting on a heliograph – last used in South Africa by the British forces in the Boer war. It had two mirrors: one focused on the sun; the other in the direction of the site one wanted to communicate with. Cellphones and even short-burst wireless transmissions could be tapped into and give away our position, so I would want to avoid them as far as possible. And in bright sunshine, the heliograph would be a better way to communicate with Moshe's undercover agent in Iraq than a conventional signalling lamp.

"I know," I said, seeing a look of consternation on Gadi's face, "very, very old-fashioned, but using this we can communicate with any given coordinates as long as we have a clear line of sight – and no chance of being listened in on." The heliograph was foolproof – only someone in the immediate vicinity could see the Morse code being sent and received.

Day after day we endured all-terrain physical training. If we were not climbing steep hills with a sand-weighted backpack on a hot day, we were doing a 30km run with a weighted knapsack in the rain. But one night, collapsing onto the top bunk after the day's final push-up and sit-up session, I realised I felt great. The two of us were reveling in a level of physical fitness we had long forgotten. My brain was brimming with information, and as the day of our departure drew nearer, I struggled to get to sleep, turning the details over and over in mind, trying to project myself into the foreign landscapes we would traverse and negotiate the obstacles we might face.

The literacy rate in Iraq was only 55 percent, so our documents will not always be meaningful, I would think, as I slid under the sparse covers. And in any interactions with the lower levels of officialdom, I would have to be vague about exactly what I was selling for the reconstruction effort. Call it confidential.

We would need money both for living expenses and for bribes where necessary, I would suddenly remember, just as I was about to drift off. Cash was king in most places, and bribery would be not merely condoned but expected in most places.

And fuel would be another problem. We would have to carry most of our own supplies, topping up wherever possible. Luckily, fuel smugglers abounded in greater Iraq, and we were sure to find a way of buying some overpriced fuel. Every night, these thoughts would crowd my mind, becoming more and more muddled as sleep overcame me.

"Remember, no heroics!" said Meyer, as we finally prepared to depart. "Get in, plant the beacons, and get out! One last thing – give me all the shoes and boots you will be taking with you."

We both looked at him as if he had gone crazy. Nevertheless, we had soon passed over our footwear, and were shoeless for nearly an hour.

When Meyer returned with our shoes and boots, he gave us a big grin. "Now the two of you are rich," he said.

"Not the way my Teva shares are going," I joked.

"Maybe not – but look closely at the heels of your shoes," he instructed. We looked, but saw nothing different.

"Now, press on the raised dot near the heel," he said. I pressed, and suddenly the heel swiveled open to reveal a cavity that glinted gold.

"Yes, each heel contains the same secret," he smiled. "There are three Kruger Rands in each one." I looked at him, uncomprehending.

"A Kruger Rand," explained Meyer, "is pure gold – exactly one ounce. At the present gold price, each one is worth over $900. They are yours only for the duration of the mission; no-one will refuse a bribe of that amount in Iraq or Iran. But don't forget, the lady in accounting will want them back when you return. If they don't come back with you, you'll have to give a very good explanation of where and how they were spent."

"Well, that's all. You two won't have an active part in any attacks and you should have no real problems."

By this time, cars were waiting to take Gadir and me to our respective departure points. Meyer waved us goodbye with a sober look that reminded us we might never see him again. "*Shalom* and *l'hitraot*," were his parting words.

Chapter 19

Sitting in the lobby of the luxurious Inter-Continental Hotel in the Jordanian capital of Amman, I hardly recognised Gadir when he walked in. Dressed in a well tailored blue suit, and sporting a red checked *keffiya*, he looked like a member of the Jordanian Parliament – not the Gadir I remembered dressed either in his casual Israeli army uniform, or in well-worn jeans and a T-shirt on deliveries to the Netanya *shouk*.

I too had been transformed; I was now the prosperous German businessman, Dieter Schumann. My Italian-cut silk suit and tie would be equally unfamiliar to Gadir, who was passing as the well-travelled Bedouin trader who shared his name by a happy coincidence.

I had not expected Gadir to recognise this well-buffed version of myself, especially in the splendid suit. But recognise me he did, and, walking straight up to me, extended his hand and said, "Herr Schumann, what a pleasant surprise to see you so soon. I had not expected you until tomorrow."

I rose to greet him. "Please, let us not stand on ceremony," I replied, "my first name is Dieter, and, if I may, I will call you Gadir. We will be together for some time, and it would be pleasant to start off on a less formal footing. I hope you will forgive my Arabic; it is not entirely fluent, but will undoubtedly improve during our time together."

We had been schooled during our special training to interact only under our mission names, and as our appearances were so radically different, it was easy to avoid slipping back into our familiar names and identities. Conversing in Arabic was also helpful; of necessity I could speak only in the formal, stilted manner my competence in the language allowed. Even if I had tried, I could not have addressed Gadi in the friendly, informal lingo that would cast doubt on our cover.

"To my regret, I speak no German, and only a little English," replied Gadir, who had taken a seat to my left. "Your Arabic is very good. We will understand each other perfectly. I am at your disposal, as arranged with our Trade Ministry, and I hope I can help you in your business dealings. May I ask your plans?"

"My hope is that we can leave for Iraq tomorrow. I have rented a Land Rover to travel overland for the journey. I will rely on you to provision us with all we will need. My company has provided a liberal expense account, but I must still account for every dinar, dollar, or mark we spend." I could not suppress a jibe at the organisation's money counters, just for the sake of it. "Accountants know only written facts and figures," I continued, "but I am sure that we will manage all right with your wise guidance."

Gadir could not supress a grin. "Dieter, I am not schooled in record-keeping, but you may rely on me to buy only what I feel is necessary for our journey. I will also make provision for any unexpected problems which we may encounter. Iraq has not yet recovered from the second Gulf War, to say nothing of the ongoing American attacks on its industrial radar sites. Because of the continuing hostilities, all Europeans are regarded with suspicion, but the Germans have not taken an active part in any of the attacks. It is my hope that you will face no major problems."

Gadir went on to propose that we take the Land Rover for a drive, allowing him to familiarise himself with the controls, and begin our provisioning at once. This was fine with me. I had flown in the previous night and had ample time to rest.

The next few hours were spent in a frenzy of shopping. There would be no supermarkets where we were headed, and the Iraqis, by all accounts, were short of nearly everything but the most basic necessities. Even farm produce was in short supply in the countryside, as the Baghdad black market paid farmers better prices than they could get locally.

Finally, we were done, and I took my leave of Gadir, who would take the loaded vehicle to a secure location. We arranged to leave the hotel for the Iraqi border at Rushweida at first light the next day.

That evening, I settled my hotel account, carefully stowing the indispensable receipts in a jacket pocket. I planned to pack my few belongings, and retire early in preparation for our dawn departure. But this was not to be.

As I entered my room, I was surprised to find a hotel maid still busy in my room. "Thank you, but that will do," I said to her back as she turned down the covers. My exasperation turned to shock when she turned around: this was the same young woman who had welcomed us at the safe house in Netanya. Putting her finger to her lips, she beckoned me into the bathroom.

"I am nearly through," she said, in faultless Arabic, "but the bathroom taps are of a new Italian design and I must show you how to operate them." So saying, she turned the taps on full. As the sound of rushing water filled the room, she put her mouth near my ear. "My name is Dana," she said. "We were never introduced. I have an urgent message for you."

My stomach turned as she continued. "There was the usual *balagan*," she whispered. "Mario and Jibril have escaped from custody – and no, we are not the authors of their disappearance. Naturally, they have skipped the country. They are not aware of your mission, of course, but intelligence suggests they have crossed the Jordanian border and might be heading in the same direction as you."

I groaned as Dana closed the basin taps and began demonstrating the bath fittings. This was a major shock; our invisibility in this part of the world was key. In fact, the only advantage Gadir and I had over experienced agents was the fact that no-one could rcognise us and put two and two together. With Mario and Jibril on the run, there was a grave threat to our cover. Life and death in an Iraqi prison was not a pretty thought. Nor was the possibility that, if caught, we would be lucky to make it to jail alive.

"What are we expected to do?" I asked, knowing it was too late to abort – especially if Mario and Jibril's escape sped up any planned attack.

"You have to decide whether you want to go ahead in light of this new development," she answered. "Otherwise, we will get you out of the country and try to make alternative arrangements."

Dana moved now to the shower mixer, reciting self-evident instructions in Arabic. "I have to speak to Gadi," I said. "Although I expect he will want to press on, this must be a joint decision. I know where he is staying and will go there now. But what about you?" I asked, concerned for her safety.

With a look of mild irritation, she shrugged off my anxiety, and I realised with embarrassment that she was undoubtedly my superior in matters of espionage; certainly not in need of my assistance. "Don't worry about me" she said, "I will meet you in the hotel coffee shop in two hours. Will that give you enough time?"

"More than enough," I said, "see you then."

Leaving the hotel, I walked a few blocks and found a late-night cruising taxi, which took me to the villa of Gadir's rich relative in a suburb near the royal palace. The place was in darkness, but there was a watchman at the gate warming himself near a charcoal brazier.

He looked at me with suspicion when I approached him, and even more so when he heard my Arabic, but the waiting taxi and a gift of *baksheesh** dinars reassured him. Telling me to wait outside, he went in to summon Gadir, who arrived cross and rumpled a few minutes later.

"It sounds like Karameh all over again," he said, with a heavy frown. Karameh was where we had first met during an Israeli raid on the PLO in Jordan many years ago. Thanks to a mistake at HQ, the raid ended disastrously, and both Gadi and I were among those fortunate enough to be wounded rather than killed.

"What do you think?" I said, "Go back or continue?"

He thought for a moment, then shook his head. "*Ein Brerah*. There is no choice. We must go on, but if we are seen all hell will break loose. We will have to take great care."

I felt the same. "Go back to bed," I said, "I'll see you as arranged in the morning."

Back in the hotel district, I waited till my taxi was out of

---

* *Arabic: Bribe or tip.*

sight before walking back to my hotel. Once there, I went straight to the coffee shop and sat down to wait for Dana.

She arrived on time, dressed provocatively in the guise of a call girl that I had ordered. I was the only one sitting there at that hour, so she walked straight up to me. "Come," she said brazenly, "let's go up to your room." Taking my arm, she led me to the elevator.

"Let's have a shower first," she said in a voice like sweet molasses as the door of my suite closed behind us. The shower taps were on again before we continued speaking.

"Gadir agrees; we will go ahead as planned," I told her.

"There is one change to the original plan," she added. "We are trying to arrange a backup team to cover your tail. It's not yet final, but if we manage to get it right they will go in as a French TV crew, filming bomb damage and starving children with the cooperation of the Iraqi Ministry of Information.

"It hasn't been easy to organise, but it looks likely to come off. You'll have to look out for them." Dana went on to brief me on recognition signs and how to mark message drops if we needed to contact them. Her crash course in basic spy tradecraft and message drops consumed most of the night. We had been through this at the Herzliya safe house, but I had never expected we would need it.

Dana slipped out of the room at 04h00, giving me an hour's restless sleep before going down to meet Gadir, who arrived as planned in the Land Rover, looking as if he had spent the last few days at a health spa.

Wearily, I climbed in beside him and we set off for the Iraqi border.

Chapter 20

Dawn in the desert is like nothing else in the world. The rising sun tinted the endless sands a rosy pink colour, as if the world was being born anew, innocent of the horrors of terrorism, war and starvation. Even the rocky shale took on a glow, and, from nowhere, a bird swept low, looking for its morning meal.

There was almost no sound at all, but for the faint swish of our tyres on the smooth dirt road. Ours seemed to be the only vehicle out this early and, looking out over the vast emptiness as Gadi drove, I saw camels here and there, grazing on minute patches of desert scrub.

Now that we were alone, we flouted the rules and reverted to Hebrew and our real names. It seemed pointless to keep up the charade with no-one to overhear us, and over 300 kilometres to travel before the border-crossing at Rushweida.

As the day wore on and the flow of traffic increased, we took more care on the road. We had been warned of the heavy-duty trucks carrying much-needed equipment to Iraq from Jordan, which for them, like us, was the easiest point of entry. It was said that the truckers all but owned the road, and paid little heed to smaller vehicles in their path.

We passed at a distance the famous City of Petra, carved from cliffs of solid red sandstone. A world heritage site of unknown origin, it is one of the world's most beautiful ruins. Even before a treaty secured peace between Israel and Jordan, adventurous Israeli youngsters used to sneak across the border to see the beautiful, deserted city. Indeed, it became an annual pilgrimage for many young people, despite the fact that they were, more often than not, caught and briefly jailed in Jordan before returning to Israel to face, in turn, the wrath of the authorities and their parents.

Seated at the wheel, Gadi filled me in on some Bedouin folklore. Apparently, the local Bedouin believed that in the rose-coloured city of Petra, there was a fortune of buried treasure guarded by a *Djinn** made of fire. One could enter only once the being's spell was broken.

According to Bedouin legend, one man succeeded in this, and used a spell to open the great doors to the treasure. But his magic was not strong enough to re-open them, and he never came out.

"*Ya-allah*, Gadi, I hope that's not an omen for us!" I said, half joking and half serious. We both knew we might not get out of Iraq alive.

Gadi laughed. "Not like you to be superstitious, Dani," he said, and pulled over so that I could take over the wheel for the final 100 kilometres to Rushweida and the subsequent 100 to Ar Rutbah, the first real town we would encounter inside Iraq.

As we got out of the Land Rover to switch seats, I started at at a sudden noise and movement from above. Glancing up, I saw a concatenation of black-and-grey carrion crows. It seemed they had been disturbed by my movement under the lone tree on which they had been perched. Cawing and shrieking, they swooped around us, furious at our invasion of their territory. I shivered involuntarily as I installed myself at the wheel.

It seemed almost no time had passed along the endless expanse of road when we suddenly saw ahead of us a long line of dusty trucks and pickups, interspersed by the occasional heavy-laden camel or car, awaiting border clearance. We had arrived at the Rushweida border crossing.

Gadir and I switched back to Arabic, rehearsing our cover identities during the long wait. There was no problem on the Jordanian side, but we approached the Iraqi side with foreboding. A diligent search of our vehicle – in which two firearms were concealed, along with a whole array of weaponry disguised as innocent items – would mean the end of our mission and possibly a lifetime in prison. Taking out our passports and folding a 10

---

* *Evil spirit.*

dinar note into each of them, I passed them over to Gadi. When our turn came, he handed them over and we conscientiously avoided exchanging nervous glances. To our relief, our passports were stamped without question and handed back to us empty. We had made it into Iraq!

"Well, it seems that was the easy part," I said, keeping to the safety of Arabic, once we were out of earshot. "Now we have to get to the Basra area to meet with our MI6 contact. What do you think, Gadi? Should we head straight to Basra, or use my heliograph" – here I cursed my halting Arabic and resorted to a phrase of Hebrew – "to contact Moshe's friend in the mountains?" I had jotted the agent's coordinates and communication windows onto a scrap of tissue, easily swallowed if need be. "We're still in the window during which he looks out for messages, and after last night's unpleasant surprise I'd like to be sure there is no more urgent news," I continued.

Gadi agreed and, after parking the Land Rover off the road and out of sight, we climbed a rocky outcrop to a large clump of bushes where no-one would see us from the road. We needed to establish a direct line between the agent's location and our own, and this was most easily achieved by transmitting from a hilltop.

Focusing the upper mirror on the compass bearing given to us by Moshe, I tapped on the key pad in Morse: TEAM SHIMON CALLING. ANY MESSAGES FOR US?

There was no reply, and I continued flashing the message for several minutes. We were about to pack up when at last we saw a pinpoint of light coming back at us. I hastily decoded the Morse message coming in. It read: SHIMON DANGER MARIO IN YOUR AREA TAKE GREAT CARE.

We resolved to drive on and take time to investigate any signs of life – if we could quietly eliminate Jibril before he made it to Natanz, so much the better. Several kilometres later, we saw the outlines of a few shacks in the distance. We drove the Land Rover into a sandy *wadi*, covering it with camouflage netting and leaves before setting off toward the structures with Gadi in the lead, carrying a sniper rifle. Of the two of us, I was the trained sniper, but being far clumsier and noisier than my friend, I trailed 50 metres behind to cover him with the semi-automatic if need be.

As we approached the shacks, Gadi halted, signaled me to stop, and knelt on the ground. I saw him rise and creep very slowly towards the buildings, and I too moved gradually forward, keeping him in sight until he entered one of the doorways without calling me forward.

"Not there," Gadi said on his return. "There was a tiny store and I went in and asked if there was a garage nearby where I could get repairs done to my car. There was not, obviously. It's a very isolated village, and I was the first stranger they had seen in weeks. They asked for news of the elections – the only radio had broken down and they don't get the newspaper out here.

"They said there is a bigger village about 15 kilometres away – also a small place with no garage, but they thought someone there might know the mechanics of cars. They had no transport at all, fortunately, so they didn't offer to drive me."

Returning to the *wadi*, we uncovered the Land Rover and headed onwards towards Basra at maximum speed. Time after time, we saw small villages and clusters of huts, and Gadi went ahead to reconnoiter each site. As the sun rose higher and the day got hotter and hotter, we wearied of the exercise, but persisted. It was taking a heavy toll on our energy, especially Gadi, who had the most difficult part of the exercise.

At last, we stopped to brew up some strong coffee from our rations, have a bite to eat and take a break. Despite the heat of the early Spring, we craved the comforting ritual and desperately needed a sugar injection.

"How much more of this can you take, Gadi?" I asked as we reluctantly finished up.

"I am older than you, but fitter," he replied. It was true: I was still the heavier of the two of us, although a lot more of my bulk was now muscle. "Besides," he said, "I am only carrying a rifle, but you have the M16."

"OK – *kadima*,*" I said, and on we went.

At last we came to a fair-sized village, and, re-energised, took even more care than usual in hiding the Land Rover. The size of the

---

* *Hebrew: Forward.*

village meant there might well be passing shepherds, or even children taking the day off and hiking around the area.

Once more, Gadi took up the sniper's rifle, and trudged wearily towards the village. Exhausted by the heat and growing glare, I tiredly tracked behind him, carrying the M16, which seemed to get heavier by the minute. I kept my distance, trying to remain unseen while still covering him in case of trouble.

In such a big village, this was not easy, and it was difficult both to follow Gadi and to cover him from a distance. I saw him enter what appeared to be the local tea house, and waited patiently behind an unfinished building.

Suddenly, a shot rang out. Hoping desperately that Gadi had spotted Mario, I ran forward.

As I entered the teahouse, I was stunned to see Gadi lying on the floor with a leering Mario standing over him, holding the rifle. He noticed me with a momentary start, but then laughed. "Ah, my two little birds with one stone," he sneered. Pointing the rifle at Gadi's head, he scowled at me grimly. "Put down that gun, Mafouz, or your little friend will get a shot in the head."

Quickly, I weighed the options. There was no way that I could get Mario before he killed Gadi – the M16 was at my waist, while his gun was touching Gadi's head. Around him was a bunch of five heavily bearded and turbaned Iraqis, who appeared to be his cohorts. Obviously, they must be a local insurgent gang – men who sent out suicide bombers, and held foreigners captive, for whom this minor showdown was all in a day's work.

If he had wanted to kill us both, he could have done so easily. Clearly, what he wanted was information and, later, if we survived, ransom money. With Mario, it was all about money, and this gave us a chance, albeit slim.

"*Beseder*, you have us," I said, "but I'll only put down my gun when you put down yours. If you shoot Gadir, I will kill you and at least one of your friends before I go down." It was almost what the American movies called a Mexican stand-off, but the edge was distinctly with them. Despite all our precautions, it seemed that we had walked into deep trouble once again.

"Tie this one up!" Mario called out in guttural Arabic, indicating Gadir, "and then we'll attend to his friend."

I cursed myself for this catastrophe so early in our mission, but realised that sheer exhaustion, and the boredom of so many fruitless searches, had left us unwary.

Soon I, too, was bound, but, apart from a few kicks and knocks, relatively unharmed. Gadi, more damaged than me, tried to grin, but a heavy boot in the face put a halt to that. We were at their mercy.

Chapter 21

Bound by ropes, and lying next to Gadi on the dirty floor of the small Iraqi coffee house, my spirit sagged. "Oh, hell," I thought. "There goes our mission before it had even started." The thought was closely followed by another: "I've been in this movie before!"

Looking at Gadi, with his bruised face and bloody nose, I was surprised to see a flicker of a smile as our eyes briefly met. I curled into myself as Mario issued me a vicious kick in the face, and guessed what Gadi must have endured before I came on the scene.

Leaning over me, Mario spat in my face – "Thought you were so smart, did you? Well, we'll see who's smarter soon."

Taking a long dagger from his belt, he put it up against my face. "Now, smart guy, I'm going to ask you a few questions. If I don't get the answers I want, I'll use this knife to cut up your little friend here. So don't try any heroics with me – he'll be the one to suffer. And when I'm finished with him, you'll get your turn." Back in Netanya, I would have considered the threats mere bravado. But Iraqi gangs allied to Al Qaeda often kidnapped foreign workers for ransom money, and killed them with little thought if they did not get what they wanted. I kept my silence.

Obviously, one of the gang understood Hebrew, for he turned sharply towards Mario, and said in Arabic, "Not so fast, my friend. This is no place for your pleasures; don't you realise that it is a coffee house? Every minute we spend here puts us in danger from informers.

"We must take them first to our safe house; then you can question them all you want. But speak Arabic, friend, not that Hebrew of the Zionist dogs. We too must hear what they say. Besides, we have many questions of our own to pass to Al

Zarquari, so don't be too clever for your own good." At the mention of the local Al Qaeda leader, my heart sank even further at the bind we had got ourselves into.

Minutes later, we were thrust roughly onto the back of their old pickup truck. Guarded by three of the raggedly dressed insurgents, we traveled for about half an hour in a direction that was, by my reckoning, north of our previous road. Finally, we arrived at an old stone-built house, which reminded me of the Tulkarim house where we were previously held prisoner. A wooden door opened, and we were once more on a stone floor, with no visible means of escape.

As soon as we were safely inside, our captors departed and I thought for a moment that we had been left all alone in our new prison. I was wrong. From another room, a giant of a man appeared. Dressed in old, stained army fatigues and steel-toed boots, he appeared to be our jailer – no one else could be seen or heard. Dirty, short-cut black hair framed his scarred face, which was almost completely flat, with ape-like nostrils and small, deep-set black eyes. A pair of thick, bushy black eyebrows made him look even fiercer and more savage. Sweet-talking ourselves out of his grasp would not be possible – he was clearly the sort who used brute force first and asked questions later.

His arms too, hung ape-like down the side of his body, ending in scarred, filthy, dirt-embedded finger nails. His gaze seemed to take in every part of us.

"Now, my children, I will show you how we treat Zionist dogs in my prison," he roared, and swung at me, hitting my ear dead-on with a huge, deafening blow. Pain exploded in my head.

Again he spoke, in a deep, raspy voice so slurred that it seemed to come from an animal rather than a man. "Ah, my two little dogs! They said that I could get lots of information from you. No-one never holds out against Ahmed! And the more you resist, the more fun for me."

With that, he delivered a vicious kick with his heavy boot, right to my kidneys. I yelled in pain, curling up into a foetus-like ball, but I still had a little strength left to play my one card.

"Ahmed! Wait!" I gasped. "Just ask me what you want to know!"

"So soon, so soon?" he laughed viciously. "No, I must still play with you a little. Then we will talk, and I will know that what you are saying is the truth!"

"I cannot talk to you lying like this," I gasped, "let me sit up against the wall so that I can breathe. I have much to tell, and it can make you rich!"

"What can you do to make me rich, you helpless piece of shit! The few dinars you had in your pockets have been taken. I will play with you and your little friend a while, and when I'm finished my boss will hear you sing for free!"

Involuntarily, I curled up to avoid his blows as he attacked me again. With my head face-down on my thighs and my hands tied behind me, I could almost reach my feet, but I knew I would have to unfurl and expose my stomach to his ruthless kicks if I was going to succeed. Arching my back until I thought it would break, I forced my bound wrists towards my feet until my fingertips found the heel of my right shoe. My progress was slow as several times I recoiled from a kick to the solar plexus.

All of a sudden, there was a sound outside the door, followed by the scraping of a bar being lifted and the grate of a key turning in the rusty lock.

"Thank *Ha Shem*,*" I thought. I knew that Basra was still controlled by the British army, and was hoping for a rescue team of English soldiers. But instead, it was Mario who entered the room.

"Aha, my big friend, I see that you have our chickens all trussed up and ready for the grill," he said with an evil smirk. "Call Jibril. They'll talk now, and while you're gone I will have a little fun of my own at their expense."

In his animal growl, the jailer told Mario that Jibril was at another safe house, out of contact. Mario wanted our jailer to fetch Jibril in his Jeep, which was parked outside, but the lumbering giant did all he could to stay and have his fun with us. After an irritable exchange, Mario left the room to demonstrate the operation of his vehicle to his sulking sidekick, who issued a final kick to Gadir's inert form as they made their way out.

"Back soon, Dani," Mario threw back at me as he walked out of the door, "I have a few personal things to settle with you!"

Hebrew: God.

My contortions had finally succeeded in freeing three Kruger Rands into my palm during our captors' peevish argument. From there, I inserted them one by one into the gap between my shoe and my sock. I reassured myself that Mario's chilling threat would be tempered by his love of money.

When he returned, Mario locked the door behind him and came to kneel next to me, drawing closer until we were almost eye to eye. Looking at his bloodshot, piggy eyes, which glimmered with eager anticipation, I knew that it was now or never.

"Mario," I gasped, "we can still do a deal that will be good for both of us."

"What deal?" he sneered, laughing stale-breathed in my face. "We'll get all the information we need out of you sooner or later, and you have nothing else to offer me," he said, jabbing me in the side with a look of contempt.

"What about $2,000 in gold?" I asked him breathlessly.

His greedy little eyes lit up, giving the distinct impression that, if there was some kind of pay scale among his terrorist comrades, he had not yet ascended very high.

"Maybe, just maybe," he said cautiously. "But first, where is it? You were both searched. I know you have nothing left to give me."

"I'm not saying anything while Gadi and I are tied up like this," I declared boldly, putting on an air of confidence. "You can try to beat it out of me, but be quick, because if I don't give it up pretty quickly your cave-man will be back and the window of opportunity will be over. You know my security background, it'll take a while to get it out of me. So think fast; time is passing. You want the gold, and we want our freedom."

For all my bravado, I desperately hoped Mario would not call my bluff. As the seconds passed, with his features still a mask of indecision, a cold dread seeped into my bones. But suddenly, his face changed. Those greedy little eyes went blank, and he tumbled to the floor beside me.

Chapter 22

As he fell, I saw Gadir standing free with a huge smile lighting up his battered features. As he laughed with the sheer delight of escape, I remembered the flicker of a smile that I had seen on his face earlier.

"How the hell…" I began, my mouth agape.

"We can talk later; lets get out of here," he responded, producing the type of small, ultra-sharp razor blade I knew as a *sakin yapani** – the kind used by handymen the world over. Swiftly, he cut through the ropes binding me, and helped me to my feet after I retrieved the key from Mario's pocket.

I staggered after Gadi through the door, my hands and legs slowly regaining their circulation. The entrance to the safe house was not far from a reed-shrouded river bank, and as one we ran for it, plunging into the muddy water, with an identical aim in mind: to escape by swimming downstream with the help of the strong current.

After some time – perhaps a kilometre of swimming with the current – we exchanged an affirmative glance and began heading wearily towards the far bank. Having pushed through a small gap in the wall of reeds, we collapsed onto our backs to catch our breath. As the hot sun revived us, and began to dry out our sodden clothes, I began to feel almost normal.

"Wow!" I breathed in disbelief. "Thanks for that miracle, Gadi. How did you do it?"

"Easy," he replied. "You Jews think gold will get you anything. We Bedu rely instead on knives." He grinned at this – we often played around with the stereotypes of Jews as acquisitive and Bedu as criminal. "I replaced the gold in the heel cavity of my boot with the *sakin yapani*," he continued. His voice sounded further

---

* Hebrew: *Small Stanley knife.*

away than normal, and involuntarily I put my hand to my aching ear. The eardrum had probably burst, I realised, and turned my good ear toward Gadi's voice.

"I started cutting my hands free while we were lying in the pickup truck," he said, "and finished the job in the cell – although with the ministrations of that brute of a warder I could only get completely free once Mario arrived. Maybe your gold helped after all, keeping him busy that little bit longer.

"Once I was free, I jumped up and karate-chopped his neck. He will be coming round by now, and I would hate to be him, trying to explain how two men, tied hand and foot, managed to escape on his watch."

For a few more moments we lay smiling in the glow of our victory. But our next challenge was already upon us: how were we going to find our way back to the Rover, where all our food and equipment was stowed? We had only the vaguest idea where we were in relation to the village we had been captured in; our compass and GPS, too, were back at the vehicle.

"Not to worry, Dani," Gadi reassured me, "it's nearly dusk, and the dark of night will help. Remember, I am a trained *gahash* – the stars will show me the way, and by dawn we will be close enough to follow the tracks to our car."

And so it was. Slowly and tiredly, I followed Gadi's steps, and by dawn we could see in the distance the little tea-house where we had been captured. We were on our way again well before six in the morning.

My favourite Adi watch had ripped from my arm during the previous day's encounter, but fortunately there was a spare in Gadi's pack. After an hour's driving over the bumpy, dusty road, we had passed Ar Rutbah and were far enough from our captors and close enough to a hilltop to risk another helio message to the lonely Mossad agent holed up there. Looking back along the route we had driven, no telltale dust clouds indicated a tail.

As we waited for the communication window to open up and looked out for a suitable hideaway for the transmission, I thought about this poor man: watching and waiting, watching and waiting, all the while in mortal danger. As our only safe link to home, and theirs to us, he was the hinge on which our whole mission rested, yet his job was far removed from the sophisticated world of British MI5 counter-intelligence 'watchers' with their massive back-up and technical support. Our guy was just a lonely, isolated old man who had dedicated his life to his country. It was a job I could never have done.

Finally, we found a good spot, and broke all records in heliograph assembly time. The little dot of light appeared on the hilltop, visible – I hoped – only to us. We quickly sent our message, giving a brief report back and approximation of where we had been held by the insurgents.

W<small>AIT</small>, came the one word reply. So that's what we did, looking around constantly to ensure that we hadn't been spotted. There were American patrols, Shi'ite rebels, and even wandering goatherds to look out for.

Finally, the distant light started blinking again: Y<small>OUR MISSION NOW TOP PRIORITY. PROCEED SOONEST TO AGREED MEET POINT WITH</small> B<small>RITISH CONTACT. YOUR CODE</small> S<small>USHI.</small> G<small>OOD LUCK AND GO FAST.</small>

Having dismantled the heliograph, we quickly re-checked our GPS position, and set an automated course. Waiting only to top up our fuel from jerricans, we drove off, following the pre-set route. Despite our fatigue, we concentrated all our remaining energy on staying alert for possible dangers.

After three hours of tough traveling, we were finally near Basra, and close to our meet point. We drove off the road at the first *wadi* we spotted, where we changed our tattered garb for khaki trousers and shirts, and camouflaged our Rover with netting and branches from the surrounding bush. We bade a fond farewell to the M16 and sniper rifle that had served us so well, as well as the heliograph – from now on, secure cellphone calls would be our only means of communication.

Just before setting off, slung on our Bergen back packs, which were packed to bursting point with rations, weapons, explosives and equipment. In our exhausted state, their weight bent us over almost double. Nevertheless, we moved slowly and silently to our rendezvous with the British MI6 agent, in a shell-battered neighbourhood in Basra.

Chapter 23

It was amazing how fit we had become. Some months ago, I would never have thought that I could carry the overweight Bergen more than a few metres, but here we were moving forward at a steady pace, stopping only to check our GPS position and take compass bearings to make sure we were still on track. Now and then, we took a few sparing sips of water from our bottles and scouted for any possible pursuers.

Suddenly, we heard a loud roar approaching from behind us. Falling flat on our faces – not easy with the weight of our Bergens on our backs – we cautiously scanned the surrounding area. To the rear, we saw a small convoy of vehicles. As it neared us, we noticed that the lead Humvee was sporting the French *tricolore*. Naturally, we wondered whether this was the backup 'film crew' Dana had promised, but how to tell for sure?

"Leave it to me," Gadi said. Slipping his shoulders out of the Bergen's straps, he crawled forward a few metres and emerged at the roadside waving a red-and-white striped flannel cloth that I realised must be his gun cloth. His arms were raised as if in surrender.

"Sushi, for the love of Allah, sushi!" he declared as the convoy reached his position.

His gamble paid off. Recognizing our codeword, they halted. Taking no chances – we had had far too many surprises up till now – I remained hidden, waiting, until Gadi gave me the all clear to join up with them.

French *tricolore* notwithstanding, the leader was an Israeli and, what was more, someone I remembered from our training course. "*Shalom chaverim,**" he said, introducing himself as Benzi, "I

---

* *Hebrew: Peace, friends.*

have news for you from Meyer. Both good and bad – as usual in the army. The good news is that you can proceed safely to your meeting near Basra. We located the safe house where you were held; found two dead bodies and an ogre of a man still alive, though a bit the worse for wear.

It seems Jibril returned, saw the two of you gone and Mario tied up on the floor, and slit the man's throat without another thought. He then turned on Taysir, the ogre, but he was simply no match for someone that size. The big guy may not even have intended to kill him, but Jibril is also out of the picture for good".

"What's so bad about that?" I asked, "it all sounds good to me."

"Wait – here's the bad news. Your mission has been made much more difficult. After you have crossed the marshes, you are to make your way to Natanz with all possible speed. Our leadership has finally decided that we can no longer wait for the UN to take action. The US is hamstrung by a divided legislature and its forthcoming presidential elections. All the while, uranium enrichment continues unabated at Natanz while we remain on the back foot.

"With Jibril and Mario off the radar, there will be confusion at all levels of the terrorist network. There's no telling what will happen after they restructure their leadership and communication channels, so all operatives will be using this window of opportunity to strike before they have a chance to reorganise.

"Obviously, there will no longer be a visit to Natanz, which is good news, since all eyes will not be on the plant in the next few days. In fact, all parties in any way involved in the tactical nuclear projects the umbrella organisation is working on will be trying to salvage the relevant operating structures in the days to come. Conveniently, that will draw attention away from the most valuable resource for terror in this part of the world – the reactors here in Iran."

Gadi and I looked at each other in disbelief. To us, the previous day's encounter had been a highly regrettable shambles. Now it seemed that we had inadvertently advanced the mission by several strides!

"As you know, three of the Gulf States have given our air

force permission to over-fly them in the event of a no-option attack on Iran's nuclear assets, and that time has come – intelligence shows they are building nuclear capability, and their regular inflammatory declarations, prevarication and delay tactics point to only one conclusion. We have been planning an attack of this sort for some time, and have been fine-tuning it in the last few months, so we are confident we can make good use of this disruption in the momentum of terrorist activity. But for such a plan to succeed we will need agents to activate the GPS markers in the tunnel under the Natanz plant. As time is too short to send in alternative agents, this task will fall to you. You will contact your controllers when you have positioned the markers, and stay in touch. The code word to activite the sensors will be 'Code Red'."

Our momentary sense of elation dissipated, as Gadi and I absorbed this change of plan. We would now be at ground zero when an Israeli strike was initiated.

The agent paused and cleared his throat, as if to distance himself from the death sentence he had just dealt us. "The office is pleased that you have managed to hold your own up till now despite yesterday's debacle," he continued. "Deliberate or not, the two of you got Jibril out of the way and created a convenient diversion in the umbrella terror network. We can only hope and pray that you will keep up the good work as you get closer to your target."

He went on to brief us for the mission going forward. "You know what you need to do, and I am now going to brief you on what we know about the site layout. This should help you navigate your way to the entrance." At this, I leaned in closer to make sure I heard every detail. With my dulled hearing, I was losing a word or two here and there.

"First," he began, "I must warn you that Natanz is surrounded by a high voltage, electrified fence, and the perimeter is rigged with anti-personnel mines and acoustic sensors. I'm sure it does not come as a surprise that it is the most heavily guarded place in Iran; only by subterfuge will you succeed in infiltrating the plant. There are six big buildings above ground, with two huge structures underground – 32,000 square metres apiece. Although the total planned is 5,000 centrifuges, there are 3,000 presently working down there.

"According to Sunni dissidents, there is an entrance to the underground structures through a narrow tunnel, where supplies are brought in via a railway. The tracks are just slightly smaller than the width of the tunnel.

"As you know, everything depends on pinpoint accuracy. The walls of the plant are two-metre thick concrete. The reinforced concrete floors and ceilings are even thicker, and can withstand all but the most powerful, and precisely-directed bomb strikes. So there is no room for error – you must place the two GPS markers right at the entrance to the underground tunnel so that we can send in aircraft carrying bunker-busters.

"Failing that, we only have second strike capability to depend on. As you will know, our Arrow anti-ballistic weapons system is now operational, but not thoroughly tested, and if even one nuclear warhead got through Israeli defences there would be hell to pay. So, for the contingency that Iran initiates an atomic attack on Israel, four Dolphin submarines are stationed not far from the Persian gulf, equipped with Cruise missiles armed with atomic warheads. For obvious reasons, we would prefer not to use nuclear weapons; we favour aborting any nuclear offensive against Israel. For that, we are dependant on your success in marking the entrance to the Natanz plant. And, if you succeed" – he cleared his throat again at this remote possibility – "one of our subs will be used as your exit route."

Chapter 24

We took a short time to digest and fully understand the implications of what we had been told. Not only were we on a virtual suicide mission, but we were teetering on the sharpest edge of an Israeli attack on Iran.

We had known all along that the mission of pinpointing the Natanz entranceway was audacious and nearly impossible, but here we were just days from sight of the nuclear fortress, and – if all went well by divine intervention – escape from a conflagration of frightening proportions. Silently, we looked out at the sparse landscape.

My mind turned for a moment to Adinah, who I would probably never see again. My eyes narrowed against the sun, still gazing into the far distance, I wiped my forehead with the back of my wrist. "Gadi," I said, slowly, "I think this will be our one last great adventure."

He made no argument. "Dani," he said, reverting to my real name, "promise me that if you are the only survivor you will personally inform my wife and children." He was still staring out at the horizon. "I will do the same for you," he said, turning to meet my eye, "I know who you would want to say goodbye to." Neither of us wanted to mention the name of the woman Shimon had left behind, and her involvement with me, his best friend. Meyer had broken that unspoken rule, but we had no intention of doing the same.

I broke away from my thoughts of impending doom to address the leader of the contact group. "Can I ask you a favour?" I said, "We've walked quite a way carrying these heavy Bergens; can we beg a lift to Basra from your lot?"

"Typical Dani *chutzpa*!*" he laughed. "Sure. But you dive

---

* *Hebrew: Cheek.*

out the minute we see a checkpoint up ahead – Bergens and all."

Hardly waiting for him to finish, we jumped into the second hummer, and stowed our Bergens amongst their baggage. The ride was smooth and easy in contrast to our journey into Iraq. It seemed their route had been carefully chosen to avoid possible problems.

We took the opportunity to relax at last. Several times, I lapsed into a doze as we trundled across the Iraqi interior. The scenery was not all that pleasant to look at – we passed through a couple of small villages bearing the marks of terrible bomb damage from the American attacks a couple of years back. There were few signs of life.

Finally, we approached the outskirts of Basra, Iraq's third largest city, situated over 500 kilometres from Baghdad. Basra had been the port from which the legendary Sinbad had set off on his famous sea voyages, and it was still the country's main seaport, with constant sea traffic shuttling along the Shatt El-Arab waterway.

Sadly, we were not here as tourists. In less charged times, I would have loved a chance to explore the old buildings and market places, and to gaze at the huge date palms, towering far taller than the ones we saw in Israel. But as it was, we were on an urgent mission, and Basra itself was hardly wooing international travelers. The city was still occupied by British troops who, to our amazement, wore soft regimental headgear rather than helmets. The feathers in the Scots troops' berets seemed almost whimsical in this conflict-torn country.

We hauled our Bergens off the Hummer at a nondescript intersection and plied our way along one of Basra's many canals. The history of the last few years made it difficult to believe that Basra had once been referred to as the Venice of the East. Following a penciled map scribbled down by Benzi, we headed for the rendezvous point with our MI6 contact. We arrived at last at the appointed place: the ruin of a jewellery store in a once fashionable area, whose beautiful buildings had been pitifully destroyed by bomb and shell fire. We marked a large X16 in the dust that coated one of the shattered windows. This was our indication that we had arrived at 16h00.

Now the waiting game began. I remembered my first staff sergeant with his constant harping on how the army was "all hurry up and wait, hurry up and wait." We began to seek out a hiding place nearby.

Our contact would be passing by the site at least once a day to look out for a sign of our arrival. As soon as he found our mark on the window, he would make his own mark beside it, which would be the signal to rendezvous at that spot within three hours.

"Well, Gadir," I said, resorting for safety's sake to Dieter's faltering Arabic, "you are the scout. It will be best if you find a place for us to lie up and see without being seen."

"Easier said than done," he replied, looking around. He set off on his own to scout for possibilities. Shortly afterwards, he returned with a grin on his face.

"Follow me, I've got just the place."

Lugging my heavy Bergen along with me, I trudged after him.

"Here," he said, all of a sudden. "Just look up."

I did as he instructed, and saw that he was pointing at the top floor of a once-beautiful home, now almost destroyed by shellfire, and obviously deserted. We climbed the ruined staircase to the second floor, and I saw that it gave us a clear view of the marked window.

"Great work, Gadi," I said, dropping my Bergen to the floor with a deep sigh of relief. I thought once again how lost I would be without his help.

We stowed our Bergens in what had once been an alcove for a built in cupboard – now just a gap in the wall. The home had been gutted of everything usable.

Taking out our sleeping bags to lie on, we made ourselves an unpalatable meal of dry, ready-to-eat military rations. Filling but tasteless, they gave us the protein we needed, and we washed the meal down with warmish water from our canvas-covered water bottles.

We had not slept for almost 48 hours, but even now we would have to take shifts to rest. Gadi took the first shift of four hours, while I watched and waited for our contact. When my turn came, sleep eluded me, and I just lay on my back, hoping that I would doze off eventually. The ache of my burst eardrum would make it difficult to relax.

Looking up at the clear, starlit sky, I began to think stargazing was one of the most beautiful experiences possible. There was not a cloud in sight, and millions of stars sparkling overhead. It reminded me of a visit to a jeweler when I first got married. He had laid out a selection of small diamonds on a blue velvet cushion, and the sky above us looked just like an endless collection of diamonds on display.

Without even noticing it, I drifted off. But it was not a dreamless sleep. I dreamed that Shimon was still with us. "Dani," he said, "we have come so far, we must continue until the end."

Then I dreamt of Adinah, and our short-lived passion. At one point I felt her near me, but when I reached out, I felt only the rubble of the floor.

I dreamed of my father, and his sudden heart attack. One moment he was with us; the next, he was just a cold, lifeless body. Somehow, a verse from Pushkin, long forgotten, learned by rote at school, entered my dream: "Past sorrow is to me like wine./Stronger with every passing year."

I awoke to feel Gadi nudging me. "Time to take your watch shift, Dani; I have let you sleep too long."

Slowly and groggily, I pushed myself upright, and patted Gadi on the shoulder. "Thanks, my friend," I said, "you also need sleep; I'm ready to take over now."

With that, Gadi dropped to the floor, exhausted. within seconds he was sound asleep.

I looked around me. The diamond-studded velvet of the sky had given way to the grey and crimson hues of pre-dawn. Below us, I could hear sounds as early risers headed for work, and lights had come on in scattered buildings. Soon the old town would come back to vibrant life, and I had a job to do.

Lying down on the rough surface of the rooftop, I scanned the spot where we had left our X on the dusty window. Still no corresponding sign that our mark had been observed by the MI6 agent. Patience had never been one of my strengths, but I forced myself to relax my body, bit by bit. Soon, I found that my mind, too, was relaxing, and much of my previous tension had disappeared. So relaxed was I that I almost fell asleep once more.

Luckily, the street had awakened and the sound of traffic drew my attention to cars and rattling trucks in the road. The shouts of neighbors yelling greetings to each other punctuated the morning.

War damage aside, it was easy to visualise what a beautiful city Basra had once been, with the graceful domes and minarets of its many mosques, and date palms towering above its residences.

On the Shatt El-Arab, where the Tigris met the Euphrates, it was still a lovely city, lush and well watered, with dhows and canoes gliding along the smooth waterways, and the constant twittering of countless birds flitting from tree to tree.

I recognised small but regal malachite kingfishers, and multi-coloured bee-eaters. Once upon a time these had been a familiar sight on the Netanya cliffside, but the towers of luxury apartments had displaced most of them, along with many other species of wildlife. The disproportionate towers had also blocked the sea breezes I had so much enjoyed.

But if we did not succeed in our mission, I would never spend lazy days in Netanya again, and with that thought I realised I had let my mind wander away from the task at hand. A slight figure in the street below was making a cross, marked 0700, near to ours. We had at last established contact. Just three hours to go before meeting near the marks. Fortunately, I had glimpsed our contact, and knew who to look out for: a slight figure dressed in white robes, and the *keffiya* worn by residents of the Emirate States.

I decided to let Gadi sleep on. We needed all the rest we could get after the rigours of the past two days. Fully awake now, I turned my attention to an ancient date palm growing nearby. After years of buffeting by the prevailing sea breezes, it had grown branches, one of which was almost touching the roof top of our hiding place. With little effort, I leaned over the roof balustrade, and, with my army knife, cut a huge bunch of ripe dates from the nearest branch.

There were more than enough of the luscious yellow dates to provide a good meal for the two of us. It would be a welcome variation on the bland rations we would otherwise be confined to.

Two hours later, I woke Gadi, told him the good news, and, to his delight, offered him a handful of sweet dates for breakfast. We ate our fill, and drank deeply from our canteens.

Morale boosted by the energizing sleep and food, we slowly and cautiously descended the damaged staircase to ground level. Gadi exited first, then gave me the OK to join him.

Although my body and mind were in far better shape than they had been when we had arrived the previous day, I felt increasingly tense as our rendezvous time neared. What if it was a trap, and we had once more been betrayed? What if our contact himself had been unmasked, and was being used as bait to capture us?"

Gadi and I had discussed this possibility, and I had offered to meet the MI6 contact alone, allowing Gadi to lie hidden nearby, until I signalled the all clear. If our contact was being used as a lure, I would be the one to be hooked.

Chapter 25

I crossed over the road. It was now 09h50 – ten minutes to go before our rendezvous. I decided to take a walk around the block in order to arrive back at the shop as close as possible to 10h00. This would also give me time to scan the area for any suspicious passersby, who might also be on the lookout for us.

There were few undamaged shop widows in the neighborhood, but wherever I saw a pane of reflective glass, I used it as a mirror to scan for anyone who might be tailing me. Nobody seemed to be following me.

The ever-reliable Adi was showing 10h00; it was now or never. With a pounding heart, I walked to our rendezvous point. At the very same time as I arrived, I saw the white-robed Arab approaching me.

My heart beating furiously with the anticipation of trouble, I forced myself to blurt: "Excuse me, sir. My Arabic is not too good. I am a stranger here, and you look like a knowledgeable man. Can you help me locate a good restaurant nearby, perhaps one that sells sushi?" He smiled broadly, and said in a clear, clipped English accent: "My dear chap, of course I do. In fact I was just thinking of heading for just such a place."

It seemed now or never. "I have friend nearby; perhaps I will call him and we can enjoy an early lunch together'?"

"I am sure that I will enjoy meeting your friend. So few new faces in this town. Call him, and I am certain we will have an enjoyable and informative meal together. Where do you come from, by the way? I can't quite place your accent."

"I am German," I replied in my best English. "My name is Dieter. Pleased to meet you." He shook my outstretched hand before I turned to fetch Gadir.

As I strode quickly back to the abandoned building, I looked around keenly for any strangers lurking nearby, but everyone seemed on the move, each person absorbed in the flow of their daily business.

Gadi raised his eyebrows as I walked in.

"Looks good, but we shouldn't take anything for granted," I said. "We are all going for an early lunch; but let's be wary in case there is something unseen around the corner."

As we joined the stranger, I sensed Gadi's tension. Although I still felt on edge, I had overcome my initial attack of nerves.

"This is my colleague, Gadir," I said, "he is a Bedouin connected to the Jordanian court. He is kindly assisting me in exploring some business prospects of the reconstruction process."

There was a momentary lull in the human traffic around us, and the white-robed man laughed as he extended his hand to Gadi. "Just call me Jonathan," he replied, winking, "I now know just who you two are. We don't really have to eat sushi, if you don't want to; I can take it or leave it!"

"Fine," I responded, "let's agree to take each other on trust. Is there somewhere we can sit, talk privately, and eat? We could do with a decent meal, and it would be good to return to some form of civilisation."

"Just follow me," said Jonathan, "I have just the place, but the way Gadir and I are dressed, we should really all speak Arabic. Yours is a little formal, but you are after all a visiting German businessman." With that, he strode ahead, and we followed after him.

Less than a kilometre away, after a few twists and turns, we came upon an undamaged building with a sign saying "Café Europa" in both Arabic and English. The three of us entered, still on the alert, and made our way to a round corner table at the back of the restaurant. It was too late for breakfast, and still too early for lunch, so we had the place almost to ourselves.

The owner approached us, bowing profusely. Turning to Jonathon, he asked, "What is your desire, O my Sheik?" Clearly this was not Jonathan's first visit.

"Not a dancing girl," said our new friend, "it's a little too early for that. All we want is a light meal, and your best coffee. I am trying to do business with my German friend here, and we would like to be able to talk without being disturbed."

"Your wish is my command," said the owner, sounding like the genie in the tale of Alladin. "I have some freshly caught sea bream, and the yellow rice you like. Should I serve that?"

Our host looked at us, raising his eyebrows in a question. Gadi and I nodded affirmatively, and the restaurateur departed.

"Right," said our host, "as I am now certain of your identities, I can reveal to you that my name is in fact Sheik Hassan al Mahmoud. Hassan will do for now."

This was most unexpected, but a little probing revealed that Hassan had been recruited into the MI6 while completing his studies in philosophy at the University of East Anglia in the UK, where he had also developed his clearly Anglophile tendencies.

"I have been instructed to help you get through the marshlands to the border with Iran," he continued, once our questions were answered. "Do you know anything about the territory?"

"Regretfully, no," said Gadir, "but I am Bedu, as Dieter told you, and come from a family of trackers. If you give us some background and accompany us to the border, I am sure that we will manage."

"It is not as easy as you think," said Hassan. "Still, we are here alone, and I will do my best to help you make the journey as easy as possible. I understand that you will be carrying some very heavy baggage, and will help you with that, but it will not be an easy task. The journey is dangerous."

Gadi and I exchanged glances; we knew what was in store.

Overhead, the ceiling fans droned, revolving slowly. Their faint noise, together with the bubbling of the *hookah* pipes at distant tables, seemed like in the soundtrack to a macabre movie, adding somehow to the drama of the moment.

We nodded our agreement and understanding of what might be involved.

"What can you tell us," I asked, "about the journey and the people we will meet en route?"

"We have time," said Hassan, "but we will have to talk whilst we eat. Let's begin with the people. They are the marsh Arabs, or Madan, as they prefer to be called. Once a thriving and innocent community, most were wiped out by Saddam Hussein. They had made the mistake of trusting the Americans, and after the first Gulf war, revolted against the Ba'ath regime in Iraq, thinking that the US would come to their aid. As we all know, that help was not forthcoming, and in revenge Saddam dammed the upstream rivers and drained the marshlands that had been their ancestral home for centuries.

"In the process, nearly 90 percent of one of the planet's most unique wetlands was virtually destroyed. The United Nations has called it one of the world's greatest environmental disasters.

"In addition to drying up the wetlands, Saddam used chemical warfare and attacks by helicopter gunships to eliminate most of the population.

"In the 1950's, around 400,000 Madan resided in the marshlands. Now, their total population is just over 40,000. For the most part, these survivors live in abject poverty in refugee camps in Iran. Another 20,000 still live in the marshes, eking out a meagre living from the few remaining pools of water, surrounded by a wasteland of cracked and salinated earth. As you can imagine, the remaining Madan, in their once-fertile home, now hate all foreigners. They blame the Americans and their allies for failing to come to their aid, and the Iraqis and Emirates for keeping quiet about their genocide.

"One person who has tried for many years to make the world aware of the collective misery of the Madan is a British Peeress, Baroness Emma Nicholson. She is Chair of the Amar Foundation, which provides them with aid and continually publicises their plight."

Hassan paused as our meal arrived. We were each served with a huge dish of steaming yellow rice, in which nestled a whole sea bream. On the side were small plates of condiments and a tabboulleh of chopped cucumber, tomato and mint with couscous.

Having lived on canned army rations since we started our training for the mission, Gadir and I could hardly believe our eyes.

"I know I said it would be a light meal," laughed Hassan, "but this is a specialty of Basra, and it would be a pity not to enjoy it during your brief stay."

Gadi and I tucked in voraciously. Never had I tasted such a delicious fish dish.

"I have a question before you continue," said Gadi, and I sensed his tracker persona coming to the fore. "I have heard that this area was once full of wildlife. Perhaps the war has changed that, but I would like to know what we might encounter on our journey. We must be prepared for every eventuality."

"Yes," said Hassan, as he pulled flesh away from fragile bones with his fork. "There were once huge herds of water buffalo, but now only a few survive. Packs of wolves still roam the area – far fewer than before – but now many of them are both rabid and ravenous. This is something you should be aware of when moving on foot."

"What about snakes" asked Gadi.

"I am afraid that they abound there," said Hassan. "Snakes almost always manage to slither out of danger. You will remember that this area, where the Tigris and Euphrates meet, is reputed to be the home of the Garden of Eden, and the original snake."

I was alarmed. The mission was risky enough without the dangers posed by poisonous snakes and vicious wolves. "What about the Madan?" I said. "Can we trust them?"

Hassan grinned at me. "Remember, I will be your guide, and most of their leaders are friends of mine. I get a lot of intelligence from those Madi living as displaced people in Iran; they regard me as a friend. I managed to arrange air drops of supplies from the aircraft which once patrolled the no-fly zone, and since the fall of Saddam, I have got supplies through to them from British forces in Basra."

By now, we had finished our meal, and knew we could waste no more time. Feeling replete and satisfied, we waited while Hassan, on his own insistence, paid the bill.

"Right," I said when he returned, "what's next on the programme? Do you have any transport available for us? We left our landrover about 50 kilometres back. Of course, if necessary we can all foot-slog our way through the swamps."

"No need," said Hassan, "my instructions are to take you by Hummer all the way to the Iranian border. I will do everything I possibly can to get you there unharmed. I hope to meet a Madan contact en route; he should be able to provide a guide to help you cross the border. You can depend on him – he hates the Iraqis and Iranians equally."

"Sounds good." I said, "Let Gadi and I get our kit from our hiding place, and meet up with you in half an hour."

"Thirty minutes," Hassan confirmed. "I'll pick you up at our original rendezvous point."

"Great – let's go," I said, getting up fom my seat. I left the restaurant followed by Gadi and Hassan. The unctuous bows of the owner sent us on our way.

Chapter 26

Taking great care to ensure that we were not being followed from the restaurant, Gadi and I made our way as quickly as we could back to the bomb-shattered building we had sheltered in the night before.

As we ascended the broken stairway to the roof, Gadi stopped suddenly. "Did you hear that?" he murmured in an almost inaudible tone. I only caught what he said because he paused to listen, then turned his head towards me.

"No," I replied, knowing that my hearing was no longer something to rely upon.

Once more, he seemed to hear the same sounds. Heel and toe, heel and toe, treading silently as we had been trained to do, we slowly and very, very quietly ascended to the rooftop to check it out. All the while, we were listening and making 180-degree scans of the environment for any sign of life.

Finally, we came to the roof where we had slept the previous night. Nothing stirred. The bomb damage had not left many possible hiding places, and we found no-one. Somewhat relieved, but keen to get out of here while the coast was clear, we made for the wall cavity where we had concealed our Bergen packs, still treading quietly.

I reached out for mine and, as I shifted it towards me, there was a sudden noise as a pack of rats exploded out from under it. I almost fell down with fright; their movement was so sudden and unexpected. Gadi could not restrain his pent-up laughter.

"Not to worry, it's only your rat friends!" he chuckled, "remember how their relations helped you in Tulkarim?"

He meant it as a joke, but I shivered, thinking again of how the huge Tulkarim rats had gnawed at my wrists and ropes, drawn to the smell of poor Shimon's blood.

"We'd better check our packs," I said, "the rats probably smelled the dates that you stuffed into your pack this morning." We hastily inspected our Bergens, centimetre by centimetre, wasting precious time.

"No sign that they got into mine," I said after checking fastidiously, "but there are claw and teeth marks where they tried." The same applied to Gadi's bag. It seemed we had arrived just in time – they could only have been there a few minutes.

With all haste, we hoisted up our backpacks and made our way downstairs. Hassan was already waiting for us, just across the road. "What kept you two so long?" he exclaimed. "We are already behind schedule." He laughed aloud at our explanation. "Where we are going there are things far worse than rats to be wary of."

Once again, a joke that filled me with foreboding. We had been through so much already, and for the sake of my morale I couldn't bear to contemplate the unthinkable dangers to come. We still had to make our way through the strange, polluted marshes, somehow cross the border into Iran, and then penetrate the most heavily guarded place in Iran. In truth, it was an impossible task for two fit but over-the-hill paras to accomplish.

Still, with God's help we had somehow survived up until now, against the odds, and were now heading towards our ultimate target. If there was no chance that we would succeed, the organisation would not have sent us on this mission, so I firmed my resolve with the thought that if we were the best chance against an Iranian-initiated nuclear holocaust, then it was *ein brerah* as usual.

In the meantime, Hassan was maneuvering the Humvee through streets choked army vehicles, busses loaded roof-high with passengers and their livestock, and donkey carts loaded with fresh produce. It was a revelation in driving skills the way he kept his cool; his white robes were as immaculate and uncreased as ever.

Hassan was guided by the dashboard-mounted GPS, which not only showed the route, but also gave continual instructions in Arabic, indicating each turn and change of direction. Finally, we swung into a dirt road where, just ahead of us, a rickety old wooden bridge crossed a broad river.

"This is a little-known crossing," Hassan told us. "It will take us into the marshlands. Don't worry, I used it last week, and it is still stable." The bridge swayed from side to side as we travelled very slowly towards the opposite bank. When we finally reached the other side, my face was bathed in sweat.

But our trials were not over. As the Humvee finally reached land, I could feel the wheels sinking into ground, and suddenly it hit me that we would be driving a precarious course through marshland peppered by drifts of sinking sand.

Changing to four-wheel drive, Hassan kept us moving forward into a scene of desolation like nothing I had ever encountered before. The marsh was coated with a white scum – the residue of its chemical contamination – and there was virtually no vegetation. Here and there stood the skeletons of dead trees, still rooted in the marsh. On some of the branches, vultures perched, their red, wattled necks and bald heads perfectly suited to the macabre landscape.

Hassan noticed me eying the scavenger birds. "There is little for them to feed on here, but every day the rotted carcasses of both animals and men float to the surface. That is their fodder, and at least it keeps this quagmire a trifle cleaner."

A miasmic mist rose from the marsh, and I gagged on the smell, which worsened as we travelled deeper into the marshland, accompanied by the whiff of rotting vegetation. It reminded me of an experiment in the school science lab, where I had once accidentally produced a beaker of hydrogen sulphide. The stink drove everyone from the classroom.

Eventually, the putrid smell of the rotting marshland began to lessen, and, far in the distance, we glimpsed the shapes of trees on the horizon. For the first time since we had left Basra, Hassan turned and smiled at us. "Seems that my navigation has not been too bad," he said. "The GPS malfunctions out here – possibly electro-magnetic forces from the military ordnance buried beneath the marsh."

I knew how difficult it could be to steer a compass course. I had once tried to steer a friend's cabin cruiser due east to Netanya and had no idea how far off course I was going until my friend asked me how my French was.

"I speak a little," I replied, bewildered at the arbitrary question. "Well," he replied, "you'll need more than a little where you're going." I had us on a course to Marseilles.

Remembering this, I was more than a little impressed with Hassan's navigation. With no visible landmarks, and an unreliable GPS, we were getting closer and closer to the tree-line. The character of the landscape began to change – we could see mud around us, and signs of vegetation. A short while later, a line of bare poles appeared, sunk into the land in parallel, and Hassan steered the Hummer carefully between them.

All this time, Gadi had been uncharacteristically silent, his face poised in an attitude of concentration. He had been studying Hassan's every movement, looking around constantly for signs to guide him if we had to return this way.

"Sheik Hassan," he said eventually, "how did you find your way, when I, a Bedu tracker, could find no signs?"

"Not easily," Hassan replied, "but remember that I travel this route at least twice a week.

"One of my tasks for MI6 is to maintain contact with the Madan, and to build up network of agents who hate both Iran and the old Iraqi regime. There are many of them who fled to Iran when Saddam attacked and almost destroyed their home in the marshlands. But instead of the assistance they expected from Iran, they were thrown into closed refugee camps to subsist on bare rations from the UN relief agencies. Far too little, since the Iranians siphon off most of what comes through for the poor Madan.

From these refugees, I have been able to recruit a small network of trustworthy agents, and I maintain contact with them and with their fellow tribesmen still subsisting here. I have even managed to smuggle out a few of them to join relatives here."

I looked at Hassan with a great deal of respect. He was far from the somewhat effete-looking fop he came across as over our gourmet lunch in Basra.

"You seem to have done the impossible!" I exclaimed, now that we had entered a landscape where we could get our bearings a little better. "I hope that there is someone amongst your agents who can guide us to Natanz, and help us on our way."

Gadi nodded in agreement, "In this desolate, godforsaken land, there is no way we will make it to our target without assistance, especially with the GPS not functioning as it should.

Only half a kilometre off course and we could well walk right into a guarded Iranian strongpoint."

"Yes," said Hassan, "but quiet now; I must concentrate on following the track. If just one wheel goes wrong even the four-wheel drive will not get us out of the marsh."

We kept silent as he drove on towards the now visible signs of habitation arising out of the marshland.

Chapter 27

Slowly, very slowly, Hassan steered the Hummer towards the land, which rose out of the marsh covered with a haze of miasmic mist, so that nothing was clearly visible.

We could see the shapes of trees as we drove closer, and for the first time in our long journey from Basra we heard the sounds of birds singing and chirping. Then, other sights and sounds became clearer. Rude log huts appeared, and we could hear the sound of dogs barking as they scented our approach.

As we neared the end of the marked causeway, human forms, too, became visible. About 20 metres from the end of the track we were confronted by a band of men, all of them armed. Some held kalashnikovs, others old hunting rifles. When they recognised Hassan, cries of welcome broke out, and some of the old rifles were fired into the air in celebration.

One older man was obviously their leader. Wearing a white turban, and clothed in an almost-new dashiki,* his bearing was proud. He had a strong jaw line and bright brown eyes, set deeply in his heavily lined tanned face. His hooked nose was so sharp that it almost looked like another weapon.

He strode forward, hugged Hassan and kissed him on each cheek. "Welcome, Sheik Hassan. Who are these visitors you have brought to our land?"

"Friends, good friends, with Allah's help they will help us all to rid the Madan of the Iranian vipers who take everything from you and give nothing in return!" Hassan responded. "I can vouch personally for them; they have already assisted me against those of Saddam's friends still holding out in Iraq."

"Your friends are my friends, and their enemies will be my

---

* *An Arab robe.*

enemies," said the leader, turning towards us. "My name is Ali; how are you called?"

When Gadir introduced himself, Ali observed: "I see that you are Bedu, we have many Bedu close to us. But who is the Nazarene?" My skin was naturally a light olive colour, so I was impressed – and a little concerned – that he had immediately identified me as the paler-skinned of the three of us.

"My name is Dieter," I answered, "and I have been tasked to help you, and all like you – Arab, Bedu and Nazarene – to rid this earth of the dangers from the mad Iranian who wishes to take over the world."

"Come!" said Ali, "first we must break bread together, and talk of things that are not for the ears of women and children. Come, follow me." So saying, he strode off.

I knew that we had passed the first test, but without the help of Hassan, we would have had no chance. I had always had a high regard for the British Special Intelligence Services, or SIS, who were second only to the Mossad in my opinion. Hassan's behavior, ever since we had met him, confirmed this. The three of us followed in Ali's footsteps.

A narrow track lay between tall date palms and thick bushes, the pathway was dry, but we could easily see that the land on either side of it was spongy marsh. Here and there, blue water lilies and bright green ferns interspersed the bush. Brightly hued birds flitted past, and I recognised a few malachite-coloured Syrian kingfishers, and vibrant green-and-blue bee-eaters. Perched high on the palm trees were egrets, and wading in the marshland I spied stately herons.

As Hassan had told us, this area was near the biblical site of the Garden of Eden, and the sheer beauty of our surroundings – especially after the poisonous trail we had followed to get here – filled me with amazement.

Suddenly, Gadi stopped dead in his tracks, and silently pointed to his right. There, slithering across the path, was a metre-long night adder. This deadly snake usually hid out amongst the stones of disused campfires, or the reeds flanking riverbanks. We silently froze, not moving a muscle until the snake disappeared away into the marsh.

Hassan broke the silence. "Not to worry, he is after the frogs you can hear croaking away in the marsh. He won't attack us unless we make a threatening move."

In spite of his age, Ali set a fast pace, and we were hard put to keep up with him – bearing in mind that one false step could lead us into the marshland. At last, we arrived in a very large clearing. Erected on the circle of hard earth was a Bedouin-type tent, made of dried skins, with a small entrance covered by a flap of what looked like deerskin.

Bending low, we followed Ali inside, and I was stunned by what I saw. The floor was covered with Persian carpets, rich in texture and colour, and brightly coloured silken cushions were laid in a circle on the floor. It looked like something out of the *Arabian Nights*. Seeing my surprise, both Gadi and Hassan laughed.

"You forget where we are," said Gadi. "Iran, remember, was once Persia, and the home of the world's finest carpets. You can be sure that these were not bought, but 'fell off a camel's back'!" Suitably impressed, I waited for Ali to make the next move.

"Sit!" he instructed, indicating the cushions.

Bending our collective knees, we sank, each of us, into a soft, brightly coloured cushion. Despite being so low on the floor, they were surprisingly comfortable. Ali clapped his hands, and veiled young women appeared, carrying platters of dates, sweetmeats, plates of pita bread, dishes of humus, falafel and tehina, mint salad and bowls of yogurt. Then came small coffee cups, which were also placed before us, and then filled with strong black Arabica coffee.

It had been dusk when we arrived in the settlement, and the Middle Eastern night fell swiftly upon us. The same silent young women now lit scented candles every few meters, and departed as silently as they had arrived.

"Welcome friends, new and old," said Ali. "First we must eat. Night has fallen, and it is time for the evening meal. After we have broken bread together, we will talk." He helped himself from the dishes of lavish food, and we followed suit. Even after our big meal in Basra, I suddenly felt hungry again – and the food was the type both Gadi and I loved best.

When little was left on our plates, Hassan belched politely – a requisite sign of satisfaction in the desert world – and began speaking in the slightly antiquated tongue they still spoke in these parts.

"Hear, O Ali, we give grateful thanks to you for this fine banquet; we will always be in your debt. But my friends and I are ashamed to say we have still more favours to ask."

"Do not hesitate to ask, Sheik Hassan. Have you not done many, many favours for the Madan people, and for me, too? What is it you desire of me and my people?"

"Ali, it is indeed a great favour we beg of you. We need an accomplished guide who can lead my two friends to Natanz, just over the border in Iran," he continued.

"I have not one, but three men who can guide you to Natanz," Ali replied, "they all know the place well. Their uncle is the imam of the Shaykh Abd al-Samad shrine in Natanz town, in the magisterial district of Isfahan. The eldest brother is a team leader from the Natanz excavation who has been on leave for the birth of a child."

Ali looked at us thoughtfully. "I imagine I know why your friends want to go to Natanz, but you must promise both me and the brothers that their actions will not harm the holy site," he said, after a pause.

"*Sheik* Ali," I replied, acknowledging him as a leader, "I must be honest; it is indeed our intention to cause the downfall of the nuclear site in Natanz – it threatens the entire world. But as I remember from our maps, the holy shrine is some kilometres from the Natanz site. If all goes as planned, only the plant will be harmed, and not the surrounding area.

"You must realise, that there is no guarantee of success in any mission. All I can promise is that if our plans proceed as we hope, only the Natanz uranium plant will be damaged."

"You are an honest man," replied Ali, "and I appreciate this fact. Let me discuss it with my three men, and I will have an answer for you before dawn.

"Now it is time for you to rest. A tent has been set aside for you. There is a difficult path ahead of you, and I will wake you at dawn with our reply. I think it will be favourable, but I must give my men the chance to think it through. Come, I will lead you to your tent."

There was a good-sized tent awaiting us, with a carpeted floor and three rush beds. Our Bergens were placed on the floor near the centre pole, beside Hassan's knapsack and laptop computer.

There was little to discuss. It had been a long day, especially for Hassan, so we performed the minimal ablutions and wearily lay down to sleep.

Chapter 28

The dawn was heralded by the chirping of a flock of bulbuls roosting in a palm tree near our tent. Their chirping was both musical and insistent – you could almost hear them saying, "Time to get up! Time to get up!" I loved the bulbul: its bright yellow splash of colour near the tail feathers; its black, crested head; and the naughty, bright-eyed look that made it seem almost human.

We rose, washed our faces in the bowls of water left near our beds, and dressed hurriedly. It would not do to keep Ali waiting. Waiting outside the tent was a small boy, dressed only in a loincloth. He had an engagingly cheeky look in his eyes as he jumped up at our emergence from the tent.

"Ali awaits you, my lords. Please follow me." He ran, skipping and hopping ahead of us, always looking back to make sure that we were following after him. He ran along a well-defined path; on either side, tall papyrus reeds waved in the slight breeze. The sun was just coming up from the eastern horizon, and the whole sky had the beautiful pink tinge of dawn. It was all so crisp and peaceful, yet my mind kept turning to the dangers that awaited us – dark thoughts subduing the beauty of the morning.

Instead of the ceremonial tent, where we had met with Ali the previous day, we now were guided to a log hut. Though the bark had not been removed from the cut logs, it was sturdy and well built. Inside was a long, wooden trestle table, with hand-made wooden stools on all sides.

Seated at the head of the table was Ali, as immaculately dressed as he had been the previous day. On his right, along the length of the table, were seated two men, wearing striped headscarves and dressed in matching cotton robes, gathered at the waist with knotted black cords.

"Welcome," Ali said to us, "here are the men about whom we spoke yesterday. They are two brothers: on my right is Farouk – he is the eldest – and next to him stands his younger brother, Ibrahim. I had hoped that their youngest brother, Hussein, could also help in your mission, but he is now far away. With Allah's help, he may still join you later."

We eyed them cautiously – our lives could be in their hands. They looked at us in turn, wondering if we might lead them into disaster.

Ali proceeded to introduce us to the brothers. Farouk looked at me and said, "Can we trust the Nazarene? Of Sheik Hassan I have heard nothing but good, and the Bedouin people often help us, but I have never worked with people from distant lands."

Gadi spoke up. "Dieter and I have traveled a long and difficult journey together; we have protected each other from all the many dangers we have met on this long road. I trust him with my life, which, indeed, he has saved more than once."

"I too can vouch for Dieter," said Hassan, the friends on whom I rely to supply and help your fellow Madan sent me to meet him and Gadir, and to guide them to your homeland."

Farouk gave me another piercing look, said nothing, and shrugged his shoulders.

I, in my turn, decided that it would be best just to listen for the time being and to leave the talking to Hassan. Gadir had apparently reached the same conclusion, and raised his right eyebrow as a prompt to Hassan – a gesture I had never succeeded in emulating.

I nodded when Hassan looked to me for affirmation. His mandate clear, he turned to the two brothers and spoke.

"We have a mission to undertake, in which you have been chosen by Ali to help and guide us. We do not ask you to do this for nothing; we will pay you in Kuwaiti dinars.

"Here, then, is the help we need. If you agree, we will negotiate a fair deal, but it is also work that I think you will enjoy. We need to secretly cross from your lands into Iran. From there, we must move under cover of darkness to the uranium plant in Natanz."

Farouk spoke up. It was obvious that, as the eldest, he spoke for both brothers: "This is very serious and dangerous work that you are asking of us. With Ali's permission, we would like a few minutes to discuss this in private."

Ali nodded. "I understand. Leave us for a while, but we need your answer soon. Return within 10 minutes."

With that, the two brothers rose, bowed respectfully to Ali, and left the room. Ali rose in turn, and addressed the three of us.

"I have no doubt that, having met the two brothers, you too would like a few moments to speak privately. There are matters which require my urgent attention; I will leave you for a short while and attend to them." So saying, he bowed to us and left the room.

I turned to Hassan. "Thanks for the reference you provided," I said, "but I was surprised at your suggestion that you will be among us when we cross the border – I thought you would be leaving us here. The Natanz mission is extremely dangerous. We are carrying it out for our country, but there is no need for you, too, to risk your life."

"It is not just for your country," he replied. "As you know, I work for the British SIS. You are on a mission under Mossad jurisdiction. Our organisations are not supposed to work together, but when the need arises…" He gave us a knowing look, and an unexpected wink, before continuing.

"I am a resident of Kuwait, which is why we will be paying our guides in Kuwaiti currency. We suffered under Saddam, and now we live in fear of Iran – the Mullahs there hate all Sunnis, and Kuwait is a majority Sunni country. Beside that, my London office has asked me to go all the way with you. The British government would like nothing better than for you to succeed, with no blame attached to them."

Gadi and I exchanged glances, and he gave me his signature eyebrow lift. I, in turn, nodded. "We are both honoured and fortunate to have you with us; your help and advice will be invaluable."

I rose, clasped his hand, and declared in my formal Arabic – which seemed for once appropriate to the circumstances – "Let us then be as three brethren, one for all, and all for one, like the fabled musketeers of old."

Hassan nodded and spoke in a low tone. "Assuming our guides agree, I will be able to take the four of you to within a few hundred metres of the border in my Hummer. From there on, until our mission is completed, we will have to travel by foot, carrying all we might need in our Bergens. I suggest that before we move on, you check every item carefully, deciding on what you can safely discard. We will have to move both with speed and with extreme care. The lighter you can make your loads, the better."

This consideration was not new to Gadi and I. We had extra clothing in our packs and would exchange our present garments for peasant gear, discarding the rest. Our portable shaving equipment had been abandoned back in the Land Rover before Basra, and the heat packs to warm food and water would be the next luxury to go.

Looking at the perfectly presented Hassan, Gadi couldn't help but remind him that he too would have to abandon even the basics of a civilised appearance. "Not only that," said Gadir, "we have to be fastidious in every respect."

Hassan interrupted with a chuckle. "I am in the picture," he affirmed. "I have all the necessities, down to the bags we crap in and bury to avoid detection. We will all smell to high heaven, but so will most people we meet. For me it will be a motivating factor: the faster we succeed in our mission the sooner I can return to my present well-groomed persona."

Gadi grinned sardonically, "And if we do not succeed, it will not matter how we smell."

As he finished speaking, Farouk and Ibrahim re-entered the hut. "We have thought long and hard," said Farouk. "What you ask of us is dangerous, but you are fortunate that my brother and I have all the knowledge you will need. We agree to help you. As for the matter of the Kuwaiti dinars, we require one thousand each, paid immediately."

Hassan looked long and hard at the two rogues. "Agreed, but it will be paid in trust to Ali. You know him well, and if we succeed in our mission, he will pay you as soon as he hears that all is well. If we do not succeed, you will be paid half. If, Allah forbid, one or both of you do not survive the many dangers, the full amount will be paid to your next of kin."

Farouk and Ibrahim looked at each other, and nodded.

"Right," I said, "now we must break bread together, drink some coffee, and plan our travels."

Chapter 29

A few minutes later, Ali joined us in our planning; he knew the area and the politics very well.

We ate pita bread and dates, and drank coffee poured from a beautiful, engraved brass pot, with a slender, elegant spout that stretched all the way from its base. We drank delicious coffee, thick as mud, from small cups with no handles. It was like getting a shot of adrenaline. My spirits soared, my mood lightened, and the whole encounter suddenly seemed bright with camaraderie and adventure, a far cry from the desperate life-or-death effort that it really was.

"Sheik Ali," I said, after we had eaten and drunk our fill, "I have – with your permission – a question to ask of you." He invited me to go ahead, and I asked my question: how had this beautiful, fertile stretch of land come to exist in the middle of the forbidding swamp?

A shadow crossed his face as he began to answer. "My friend, once all the swampland was like this, with tens of thousands of my countrymen living happily. You know, of course, that the cursed Saddam Hussein – may his body rot forever in hell – drained the swamps, and tried to poison what was left?"

"That I know," I replied, "and I have heard too, of Baroness Nicholson, one of the few who tried to bring your plight to the world's attention. But what I do not understand is how your beautiful habitat survived the catastrophe Saddam brought upon it."

"It is Allah's will, my son," Ali said sagely. "You remember the great Euphrates River? Well, before it joins up with the Tigris near Basra, one part travels underground, and, like a coiled dragon, surfaces from time to time before it empties, still underground, into the Persian Gulf.

"We live now on one of those pieces of land where the Euphrates rises. Its sweet waters surround us, nourishing this island as of old, and giving us pure water not only to drink and water our flocks, but to feed the blessed palm trees, which bear dates that help sustain us. Many birds nest in the palms – a feast for our eyes and ears, and sometimes a welcome addition to our diet."

"Thank you, *sheik* Ali, for your scholarly answers, but also for your help and warm hospitality," I replied.

"I, too, would like to add my thanks," said Gadir, "and now, as evening approaches, we have time before prayers to discuss and plan our heaven-ordained mission."

Hassan nodded approvingly. From his ever-present case he extracted a large-scale map, showing the Iraq/Iran border, Natanz, the land as far as Teheran to the east, and, to the west, the Persian Gulf.

Hassan continued: "Now, Farouk, we look to you and Ibrahim to advise us on the best route to take to reach Natanz. Also, how and where we can best cross the border."

Laying the map on the planked table, he weighted the corners with our brass cups, and, taking a pencil from his case, made a cross on the map.

"Here is the land of *sheik* Ali," he said, pointing to the cross he had just made, "and here" – making another cross – "is Natanz." Iraq was coloured dark red, and Iran in Green, with the blue Persian Gulf a clear boundary between the two.

"How, then, would you advise us to travel?" asked Hassan. "We can all go together in my Hummer, but it must be left hidden and well concealed, at least one kilometre from the Iranian border. From there we will travel on foot, carrying what we need in our Bergens and sacks, until we have reached our destination. Then, with the help of Allah, we will succeed in our mission and escape."

Farouk and Ibrahim looked at the map, then spoke for a few moments in low tones. Taking the pencil from the table with a grubby finger, Farouk made his own mark on the map.

"Here is where we leave your Hummer," he said, then drew a curved line to the border, where he drew a second mark, "and here we cross the border. As you can see, the line I have drawn is not straight, but it evades the check posts that the cursed Iranians have set up – even inside Iraqi territory.

"Besides the check posts, there are trip wires, which trigger explosives and transmit a warning signal to the main border posts. My friends and I often have to cross the border, so we know the route well, but we must take care. Those sons of Satan are not oblivious to our efforts to evade them. We will have to crawl on our bellies, like snakes, to escape their attention, and be sure not to disturb the environs.

"Your Bergens could be a big problem. You will need to lighten them as much as you can, and one of us – most likely Ibrahim, who is smaller than me – will have to travel last in line to sweep away the signs of our passage with his hands."

"I thank you, Farouk," I said. "My comrade, Gadir, is a trained scout, and I suggest that you and he work together to plan our movements. I value your local knowledge, but Gadir can follow a track that no one else can see, and I am sure that the three of you can plot out the safest route together, making sure that we remain unobserved."

Hassan was beginning to look impatient; it was almost time for evening prayers. "Come," he said, "I suggest that Farouk, Ibrahim and Gadir plan the journey fully, and that you and I, Dieter, plan the final details of the mission. The sooner we make our move, the better. My news is that our mission is now of ultimate priority. Every minute counts."

The others nodded respectfully as he rose from the table, but Ali broke in with a final interjection. "Before the light is gone, I must take your photographs," he said. "They will be needed for your covers in days to come." We looked askance at Hassan, but he waved away our concerns.

"Let us return to our tent," he said to me once Ali had snapped the two of us, "I must take a short time for evening prayers, but in the meantime you can draw up a list of the most important items in your kit. Those that we do not need to complete the mission will be left behind with Ali. I am sure that he can use nearly everything that we see fit to leave."

"We think alike," I said. "I have already thought through the list of things we need to take with us, but considering the need to leave no trace of our passage, I will try and cut down even further."

A congenital over-packer, I found it hard to cut down on our supplies. After all, it was almost impossible to decide under what circumstances each item might come in handy. Fortunately, the GPS was fairly small, and I had a less advanced one on the cellular phone that Hassan gave me as "a gift from MI6" when we left Basra. Besides helping us to navigate, it gave us coded text messages and a video-cam that we could use to transmit details of our progress and, hopefully, pictures of Natanz, to the hovering Eros intelligence satellite.

Night was almost upon us by the time I completed the revised packing list. No sooner had I done so than Hassan appeared at my shoulder.

"I have prayed long and hard for the success of our mission," he said, "but prayers are only answered if those that pray do all that they can to help the Almighty. I have news for you: my 'masters' in Century House have contacted me, and there is a slight change to our plans."

"Just how slight?" I asked, my automatic skepticism coming to the fore. "My experience with HQ wizards is that plans changed at the last moment almost always go wrong."

Hassan chuckled, "I agree, but when you hear what the change is, I am sure you will agree that it is justified."

The main objective remained the same: the destruction of the Natanz uranium plant. However, we were now to take a detour via the town of Natanz, and one of the most beautiful mosques in Iran.

"It is housed in the Shaykh Abd al-Samad shrine complex," said Hassan, "and existed there before those sons of Satan decided to build their atomic warheads. Perhaps at first they believed the mosque would provide them with some sort of cover.

"Be that as it may, the leading Iranian nuclear engineer, Mossen, will be there in the next few days, both to deliver a lecture to the scientists of Natanz and to receive a blessing from the Imam of the Mosque – a man purported to possess miraculous powers.

"Our task is to dispose of Mossen – he is the top scientist in the country, and, without his help and knowledge, Iran will be very hard pressed to recreate the Natanz atomic site."

"Dispose?" I said, "Does that mean what I think it means?"

"I'm afraid so," said Hassan, "but it must be done quietly, with no fuss or bother – let him simply disappear. He is known to have an eye for the ladies, and if he is missing for a short time his colleagues will think that he has slipped off to yet another illicit rendezvous. Of course, if we have no alternative we may need to take his public appearances as our only opportunity."

"And just how will we accomplish this slight change to our plans?" I asked.

"That, I'm afraid, will be my headache," said Hassan. "Headquarters has given me a blueprint, and I think that, with a few refinements here and there, we can get the job done with as little time wasted as possible.

"Now we must see how our friends have progressed with the entry plan. As soon as we have approved that, you, me and Gadir will fully consider the details of 'Plan B'."

Chapter 30

Night had fallen, and in the clear the stars shone like diamonds. The new moon appearing over the horizon somehow presaged a change in our fortunes – I prayed that this augured well for us. All around, I could hear the high-pitched singing of crickets, and the deep croaking of bullfrogs. Apart from those sounds there was an eerie silence in the encampment.

Soon, we reached the log hut where we had left Gadir with our new recruits. I opened the door and saw that their discussions had ended: Farouk and Ibrahim sat apart from Gadir, speaking to each other in low tones, while my friend sat alone at the head of the table. Obviously, all was not as well as we had hoped.

Hassan took the initiative. "All goes well, I hope? Have you three agreed on a plan?"

Ibrahim gave Gadir a black look. "Yes, we could have had a plan, but this Bedu continues to find faults. Nothing in life is perfect; there are always chances one must take."

Hassan smoothed over the ruffled feathers. Smiling, he asked, "Please tell us of your plan; I am sure that it has merit, since it is you two who live here near the Iranian border. After you have spoken, we will ask Gadir what faults he finds with it."

I glanced at Gadi, and saw him give a small nod. From the look of his face, there was no serious divergence in their views. But he was always a perfectionist when it came to plans that presented unusual dangers. We had so often been the victims of bad planning.

It was now my turn to help bridge the gap. "Speak on, my friends," I began, launching into my stilted Arabic once again. "I am sure that we can soon reach an agreement. Night has fallen, and we must leave before dawn. Our mission is now even more urgent, and time is short."

Farouk spoke up. "Here is our plan; it is simple and easy. I will tell it to you, and you can judge for yourselves.

"As you know, the border is but 15 kilometres from here, and we plan to travel together in Sheik Hassan's Hummer.

"Two kilometres from the border there is a suitable hiding place in dense bush, where we will leave the vehicle. We will very slowly creep forward, in some places on our bellies, until we reach the border fence. Ibrahim will remain behind and make his way on known smugglers' tracks to the border check post. There, he will bribe and distract the guards, giving the four of us a window of opportunity to enter Iran."

"And just how do we accomplish this?" asked Hassan.

"Quite simply" replied Farouk. As he spoke, I noticed for the first time the cast in his left eye, which gave him a rather saturnine appearance. "There is an animal called the nutria – something like a giant rat – that often crosses the border in search of green plant roots, its main food. The nutria knows no borders; when it comes to a fence, it simply burrows under and leaves a narrow tunnel behind it. We know of such tunnels along the border fence, and one around 500 metres from the check post, which our friends sometimes use to cross into Iran."

"I too know of the nutria," I said, and then bit my tongue, concerned that this would give away a more detailed knowledge of the area than my German persona should by rights have. I had friends who lived at Kibbutz Ma'ayan Tzvi, and many nutria foraged near their fish ponds, causing much grief with their destructive eating habits.

"I think I have seen these nutria on roadsides near my area," said Gadir, "but I have never seen their burrows. I remember them looking a little like squirrels, but with a very thick fur."

"Yes, that is the Nutria," I replied. "It is a rodent, but looks nothing like a rat. Its eyes are like those of a child's teddy bear. The travel guide I saw it in" – I said, quickly covering myself – "said their burrows are far larger than one would expect."

"Well, that puts my mind at rest," said Gadir, "I would never have thought that they could burrow so deep and wide that we could crawl in their tracks." But I could see that Gadir was still not fully satisfied.

"Have you any further observations to make, my friend?" I asked.

"One important one," answered Gadir, "we must time our crossing at the best possible moment, when the border guards are most distracted by Ibrahim. No one can give me the answer to that – how we know exactly when to cross under the border wire.

"Remember, we will be dragging the heavy Bergens with us. How ever silent we are, there will be some slight noise and possible movement in the fence."

"Gadir's point is well made," said Hassan. "Has anyone got a solution to this obvious problem?"

Ibrahim and Farouk hung their heads; clearly, this problem was what had caused the most antagonism between the brothers and Gadir. Their casual attitude reminded me of the Israeli *shiputsniks*,* who refurbished houses and apartments – always working without an exact plan and hoping that everything would come out right in the end.

"Let us pause and think together," said Hassan, "the plan is excellent, but Gadir's objection is a valid one. How can Ibrahim let us know exactly when we should cross?"

An idea began to form at the back of my mind. "Tell me, please, Farouk, how Ibrahim plans to divert the attention of the border guards?" I asked.

"He will pose as a peddler, and offer them bargains on his merchandise," Farouk responded. "Among the merchandise will be something sure to distract their attention from their duties: a collection of pages from old editions of Playboy magazine – strictly banned in Iran."

"Would a peddler, by any chance, also sell torches? Especially those new ones that work without batteries?"

Farouk smiled for the first time, "I see where you are heading, O Nazarene. Yes, those would be a good item to sell. With luck, Ali might have a few in his store room. Let us ask him."

He was up like a flash and off to Ali's room. He returned,

---

* *Hebrew: Handymen.*

smiling once again. "He has about 10 of them for emergencies, and is willing to sell us a few for our purpose."

"Right!" said Hassan. "We have the plan, and time is short. We must cross the fence and be well into Iran before dawn."

Gadir and I ran back to our tent, and hastily repacked our Bergens. With lighter loads to carry, we returned to the hut, where Hassan was talking to Farouk and Ibrahim.

"It is agreed," he said, "we leave within the next 10 minutes. I have already given Farouk and Ibrahim their down payments."

In our absence, the three of them had refined the details of our plan. "About 15 minutes after we leave the Hummer for the fence, Ibrahim will be at the border post, talking to the guards," said Hassan. "By this time, Farouk will have led us to the hidden nutria tunnel, and we will await Ibrahim's signal: a flash of light in the sky as he demonstrates his torches. As soon as we see that, we crawl under the fence. We follow the nutria trail, and after another 15 minutes of crawling we will be out of sight and earshot of the border guards.

"We will then be able to walk, carrying our packs, until we reach the place where Ibrahim will rejoin us. I have contacts who will assist us once we reach Iranian territory."

Without further ado, we climbed into the Hummer, and Hassan drove silently through the night.

Chapter 31

A few minutes later, Farouk tapped Hassan on the shoulder and pointed to a thick patch of undergrowth. Hassan nodded and motioned for all of us to exit. Then, under Faoruk's guidance, he steered the Hummer into the central hollow, where it was obscured by thorn-bearing bushes.

We moved forward as one, as silently as possible. Farouk signaled when we came to a furrow in the grass – the trail left by the nutria. Another hand movement, and Ibrahim left us to head for the border post with his peddlar's wares in his knapsack.

Farouk led us into the furrow, followed by Hassan, and then me, with Gadir bringing up the rear. He had the difficult job of covering our trail, but was fantastic as usual, moving each blade of grass back to its original place. Looking behind me, I could see no signs of our tracks.

Finally, we could see ahead of us the electrified border fence. Once there, we stopped and regained our breath, still lying flat on our bellies. All we could do now was wait for the flash of light from Ibrahim's torch.

As we lay there, time seemed to come to a complete stop. We lay deathly still; the slightest sound could be heard by Iranian patrols, or even at the border post just half a kilometre away. We knew that if Ibrahim succeeded in diverting the attention of the guards, we would have only a few moments to crawl under the fence. I willed Ibrahim to hurry up, and after what seemed an eternity – but was probably only about twenty minutes – we saw a beam of light flash into the sky.

Keeping our heads and stomachs flat on the ground, we wriggled slowly along the nutria's track and under the fence, pushing our flattened Bergens ahead of us.

As we moved excruciatingly slowly along the furrow and under the fence, I held my breath, fearing that a stray wire would catch on my gown, but there were no calamities. A few moments later, the four of us were stomach-down on Iranian territory – my mother's homeland, yet now a place of darkness that threatened to obliterate my beloved Israel. I gave silent thanks to God that we had made it so far.

The end of our journey was in sight; at once so near and so far. Though we were only a few kilometres from our target in Natanz, we still had one more mission to fulfill before we reached our ultimate destination.

Farouk now rose to a crouching position, and the three of us followed his example. Still crouching, he moved slowly and silently forward. None of us dared to stand upright, or to speak, but metre by metre we followed in his footsteps. With our Bergens once more on our backs, progress was painful to say the least, but having come so far we knew that discomfort was the least of our worries.

We must have covered about five kilometers like this, our thighs burning with pain, when Farouk beckoned us towards him. He signalled for us to sit beside him and, putting his finger to his lips, pointed to the east.

At first, I could not make out a thing, but after opening and closing my eyes several times to improve my night vision, I finally saw what he was showing us. There, in the light of the false dawn, we could make out a small column of men – obviously an Iranian patrol – moving in a path parallel to ours.

Once more, Farouk put a finger to his lips and motioned us to life flat on the grass scrub. It was a pleasure to comply: an opportunity to stretch out our legs and gather our strength. The false dawn told us that the sun would be above the horizon within an hour. Before that, we had to find a good hiding place, and rest up before making our way to the Shaykh Abd al-Samad shrine in the town of Natanz.

Finally, the patrol was finally out of sight. Hassan spoke up. "We have done well, my friends; now we must rest for a few moments, and plan the way forward."

Farouk turned towards him. "Only a few kilometres from here, there is an old hut used by shepherds only during the winter rains. That is where Ibrahim will meet up with us. We can rest there."

"Pardon me, O Farouk," Hassan apologised, "I should have known better; it is you and your brother who are leading us, after all."

At this, Gadir spoke for the first time. "Farouk, you have done very well, and I say this as a trained Bedouin scout. But I must correct Hassan. You are guiding us, and without your help we could not have reached Iran safely, but know this, and know it well. Sheik Hassan is leading us, and it is he who will give orders. My German friend and I also have a mission to fulfil and the necessary decisions will be made by us."

Hassan intervened. "Farouk, Gadir, let there be no more squabbling between you. You are both grown men. We have broken bread together and everything depends on our working together as one family."

Farouk nodded sullenly, and he and Gadir clasped hands.

Slowly, very slowly, we continued to make our way forward, with every fibre of our bodies alert for the Iranian patrols. The Bergens seemed to weigh more at every step; our slow pace seeming to add to their weight. At long last, just as the rising sun lit up the banked clouds on the horizon, we saw silhouetted against the pink skyline the shape of the hut we had been heading for.

Concealed from view, we were able to shrug off our Bergens and lie down on the hard earth floor, which felt as good as any luxury hotel bed. After Hassan and I had used our secure cellphones to report back to our respective controllers, he took the lead as usual. "It's good to rest," he said, "but even more important to keep alert. Remember where we are; one of us must be on watch at all times."

"I'll take the first watch," I said. "If each shift is three hours, we will all have a chance to sleep, and will be ready to move on as soon as night falls." Everybody nodded assent. But I had not yet had a chance to take up a position when we heard a sound nearby. Instantly we were all on the alert, weapons drawn.

The sound came closer, and all of a sudden we could make out the figure of a turbaned man near the entrance. Farouk gave a low laugh. "Behold, my friends, my brother Ibrahim has arrived as promised." He took a few steps forward, kissed Ibrahim on each cheek, and clasped him in a fraternal embrace.

"Welcome back, my brother. All is well, I hope? What news have you for us?"

Ibrahim looked around the hut, and, having recognised all its occupants, spoke at last. "The news is both good and bad," he said. "The good news is that I had no problem going through the border post, though my entire stock of torches and Playboy pictures was taken in payment of an 'entrance tax'."

"And the bad news?" queried Farouk.

"The bad news is that a general alert has been declared. Israeli and American politicians have been making war-like statements, threatening Iran on national television, and the Mullahs are taking them seriously. Reserve units have been called up, especially to guard and patrol the area around Natanz. It will not be easy to get into that town."

Having delivered his bad news, Ibrahim sank down on his haunches, awaiting our reaction. Gadir, for once, was the first to speak out.

"Although this is news, it is not unexpected," he said. "Not one of us thought that we could simply stroll into Natanz. Dieter and I have trained very hard for this mission, and we know what we can expect. Nevertheless, your news is invaluable. Alert as we have been, we must now redouble our efforts to disguise our true intentions."

Hassan agreed: "The two of you have done great work in helping us to get through the border. Now we need your help and advice in accessing Natanz. We will advance with even greater caution, but advance we must. Our missions must succeed at all costs, there is too much at stake for them to fail."

With that, we decided on the watch schedule, and a few minutes later I was alone at the entrance to the hut. I sat there listening to the night sounds as dawn approached: the barking of the wild dogs, and the mournful cries of the jackals, allied to the occasional hoot of an owl, and the piping noise of the nightjar.

Also in the background I could hear the incessant chirping of crickets and cicadas, and from far away the mournful croaking of bullfrogs. Lulled by the music of the night, I almost neglected my duties and dozed off, but suddenly another noise interrupted my reverie. It was the unmistakable sound of a half-track vehicle coming towards us.

Chapter 32

My heartbeat went into overdrive. How could the Iranians have found us so quickly? Was it possible that one of our calls had been intercepted, allowing the Iranians to plot the coordinates of our hideout? But neither of our calls had been over a minute, and the phones were supposed to be 100 percent secure and undetectable if used for calls under 90 seconds.

As the clattering noise of the half-track drew nearer, I concluded that Iranian technology must be better than ours. I had to warn the others. But, as I moved back into the hut, Hassan suddenly appeared before me.

"I was expecting this, Dieter. Don't panic. Just wait here with me." He grasped my left arm, and I flung it off with a sharp movement.

"I have to alert the others," I hissed urgently.

"Trust me! I have been waiting for this. It's a special delivery."

I was worried, but decided I had to trust him, for better or worse. After all, he had met us using our code word. I said nothing more, and waited beside him as the vehicle approached, slowly navigating the steep, rocky terrain. When I looked over nervously at Hassan, his aquiline features were set in a slight grin – unusual for him. The smile became broader when he noticed my glance.

"Not to worry, Dieter – or shall I call you Dani?" he quipped. I grinned back. Surely to know my real name he must be fully in the loop.

"Tell me about the half-track," I said. It was only about a hundred meters away, and I could now make out three huddled figures in the space at the back, uniformed, with turbaned heads and scarves around their faces.

"You can see they are dressed like Revolutionary Guards," said Hassan.

Warning bells rang out in my mind again. The Revolutionary Guards, known to me as the "Al Quds" brigade, were the elite force of the Iranian army. Fiercely fanatical, they were the elect troops of the Mullahs who ruled the county. But I knew that, with Hassan, nothing was what it appeared to be.

"Great,' I said, a little sarcastic, "will they stay for coffee?"

"They are the answer to your prayers, Dieter. With their help, we will get into the Shaykh Abd al-Samad shrine complex, and besides that they are making a special delivery for us."

By now the half-track was upon us. The noise had woken the others, and Gadir, Farouk and Ibrahim were suddenly at the doorway, weapons at the ready.

I motioned to them to hold their fire as the leader of the group approached Hassan.

"Greetings, O Sheik," he said, "we are here as promised, and have brought your package, as requested."

"Greetings, O Behrouz," answered Hassan. "Now meet my companions: the Nazarene is Dieter, and his companion and good friend, the Bedu, is named Gadir. Farouk and Ibrahim, if I am not mistaken, you have met before."

Behrouz proceeded to introduce Farid, Jalil and Atash, the three turbaned passengers who were now standing alongside him. They said nothing, merely nodding in turn as he mentioned their names. Their faces remained hidden by their face scarves.

From my mother's Farsi, I knew at the very least that their names were auspicious. Behrouz meant fortunate, or lucky; Farid, "unique", Jalil, "great" and Atash, "fire." If their names were anything to go by, they would be ideal for our mission.

"These brave men are all members of the Mojahedin-e-Khalk," said Hassan. "As you know, they are fighting fiercely against the Mullahs and Ahmidenijad."

I remembered our briefing back in Tzal'aim, where Yeshiyahu had told us of the work of the Iranian resistance, and their many successes. "It is an honour to receive the assistance of such brave men," I said, "Who better to help us infiltrate the Shaykh-Abd al Samad complex?"

"Indeed," agreed Hassan. "They put their lives on the line nearly every day. Because of their successes, the Revolutionary Guards have learned to change their security passwords on an almost daily basis. Fortunately, however, the Mojahedin-e-Khalk have infiltrated the ranks of the Guards. More often than not, they know the passwords in advance."

Behrouz now joined the conversation for the first time. "There are days, however, when we are not so fortunate, and if our comrades are captured and tortured they are forced to betray what they know. Because of this, we have learned to work in small cells of no more than 10 men at a time. What you see here," he said, a sweep of his arm encompassing the other three men and their vehicle, "is the minimum we need to make your mission succeed. Should we fail, our comrades in the movement will move to other locations. Their work will continue."

Hearing this, spoken in a very quiet Farsi, I felt humbled and sad. Though Gadi and I were also risking our lives, we had great backup, and contacts who could provide us with men like Hassan and his network of friends. The cells of Mojahedin-e-Khalk, on the other hand, were on their own, with almost no outside help, risking their lives on a daily basis. For an instant, I remembered my high school history teacher's penchant for quoting the Latin tag *"Dulce et decorum est pro patria mori,"* especially when he spoke of the heroic days of 1948 and Israel's war of Independence. Translated, it meant: "It is sweet and glorious to die for one's country." Each of us on this mission consoled ourselves with similar thoughts now and then, but, in truth, I knew that there was nothing sweet or glorious in seeing my wounded and dying friends screaming in pain on the battlefield.

Gadir spoke next. "Dieter, I know no Farsi; can we not speak in Arabic, or even English?"

Hassan laughed. "Gadir, I sympathise with you, but it is easier for our comrades if we speak in Farsi. If you concentrate, you will find there are many words that are similar to Arabic, and Dieter can fill you in on the details as we go." Turning to me, Hassan added, "Don't you want to know what is in the surprise package they brought for us?"

In all the excitement, I had almost forgotten the "special delivery" wrapped in hessian in the back of the half-track. Over hearing Hassan, Behrouz motioned to Jalil, and together they lifted an obviously heavy package from the vehicle. As they started to unwrap it, I suddenly realised what it was, and, to my dismay, who would have to use it.

It was a Haskins heavy-duty sniper rifle. The IRA had used them when they fought the British in Northern Ireland – very effectively, from what I had heard. The Haskins had a long, very thick barrel, designed to fire huge 50 mm rounds, each over 15 centimetres long, which had to be hand-loaded one at a time. In the hands of a trained sniper, the Haskins was accurate up to a distance of one kilometre.

I picked it up to take a closer look. Way back, I had earned my sniper's arm-patch of a long rifle. It had taken years of practice at rifle ranges to qualify, and, once learned, the sniper's art was not easily forgotten. The rifle was manageable but heavy; it must have weighed over 10 kilo's. A sound suppressor had been fitted to the muzzle, though it was not possible to completely silence a weapon of this size. In addition, a high quality optical sight had been fitted above the barrel.

Taking it down to the ground, I was pleased to see that, beside the two-pronged rest under the nose of the barrel, there were also two hydraulic shock-absorbers at the end of the skeletal stock. These would help cushion the massive recoil. A memory flashed through my mind of the ex-South African paratrooper who had told me about the first time he fired an 'elephant gun': the recoil nearly knocked him over, and his shoulder was bruised for weeks.

"Obviously this is for me to use," I said, looking up at Hassan, "but why a Haskins? It's so big and clumsy. Why not the Russian Dragunov?"

"The Dragunov is a good rifle," said Hassan, "but it's only accurate for about 300 metres. As I am sure you know, the Haskins is accurate over nearly a kilometre in good conditions, meaning you can hit your mark at a safer distance." He went on to tell me that Mossen's open-air address outside the mosque the following morning was our only opportunity given the urgency of the second and final part of our mission.

"Fine," I said a little grudgingly, "but I will need some time and space to fire it and sight it in." Every rifle had a different trajectory, and I couldn't ignore the fact that even the most minute variation could make the difference between a hit and a miss. Firing the rifle out here could attract attention, but there was no alternative. To have any chance of success, my aim had to be dead accurate – literally.

Hassan and Behrouz put their heads together, and moments later Hassan had the answer. "Behrouz suggests that you and he take a short trip in the half-track with the targets that came with the gun. There is a rocky field a few kilometres back towards the border fence. It's deserted, because animals can't graze there, and far enough from here that if the sound of your shots draws the border guards' attention, it will lead them away from our hideout rather than towards it. Of course, with the silencer on the patrol may take any noise for the sound of an unlicensed hunter shooting small deer. Behrouz will be your marker."

"OK, lets go," I said, hefting the Haskins into the half-track along with a belt of six .50 bullets. We soon reached the spot, which was deserted as predicted. Behrouz jogged down a slight hill, and set up a target. I waited until he was about 50 metres from the target before propping the Haskins on it's bi-pod stand. Then I loaded one of the huge bullets into the breech, lay down, and sighted the man-shaped target through the magnified optical sight until the cross-hairs were on the chest area.

I inhaled and exhaled a few times, relaxing as much as I could. Then I slowed my breathing, and, very slowly and gently, squeezed the trigger.

Even with the noise suppressor there was a definite booming sound, but on the plus side I hardly felt the recoil. At my 'safe' signal, Behrouz jogged to the target and placed his hand on the belly of the cardboard figure. I had centered the shot pretty well, but needed to hit about 20 centimetres higher. I clicked the sight up a little, waited until Behrouz had moved far enough away, and fired again.

This time, a flock of pigeons ascended suddenly, and wheeled away to the east. The noise was bad, and there was nothing I could do about it.

Again, Behrouz went to the target, this time putting his hand near the figure's neck. Once more, I adjusted the sight, this time one click down. I loaded another cartridge into the breech, and, once Behrouz was back in position, fired again.

This time, Behrouz put his hand on the heart of the target. Perfect. I motioned Behrouz back to his spot, and fired one more round. Again, my marker indicated the heart, but this time he picked up the cardboard target and came back to where I was lying.

"Enough!" he said, "We could wake the dead with that noise. You have sighted in the rifle; now let us return to the hut." He was right. I lugged the Haskins back to the half track, and no sooner had I tumbled in than Behrouz was off at full speed.

As we got going, I wondered why the half-track seemed louder than before. Behrouz thumbed to the rear. It wasn't the half-track, but a whirring above the hum of our engine. There, coming up out of the sun, was the unmistakable shape of a helicopter.

Chapter 33

I thought furiously. With the .50 rounds of the Haskins, and a bit of luck, perhaps I could bring down the chopper. This seemed our only way out. But before I could get the gun up and ready, Behrouz grabbed my right shoulder.

"No!" he hissed, "he is one of ours". It delayed me just a moment, but long enough that it was too late to aim and fire.

"Are you sure, Behrouz? How do you know from this distance?"

"Look up! See, he is waving to me." He was right. The pilot had upped the Plexiglas canopy and was indeed waving to us.

"But how the hell can you be sure?" I yelled into the noise.

"He's waving an orange scarf," Behrouz shouted back, "that's our sign."

No sooner had he said this than the helicopter dipped down and banked off to the south, its deafening roar dwindling into a distant hum. This was quite a relief – with one deaf ear, it was almost impossible to communicate over that intensity of sound.

"How did he know where we were?" I asked, once the helicopter had vanished into silence.

"I called him as we left this morning; he was watching over us," Behrouz responded. "Once he saw that all was OK, he resumed his 'training flight' and returned to base.

"There seem to be many of you," I thought aloud.

"Not so many," he said, "Altogether, just over 1,000, but we are all dedicated, and willing to die for our cause. If one cell is discovered or betrayed, only 10 of us will perish: there is a cut-out who acts as our contact, and he has no direct connection to us. I only know his voice, and his code word."

There was silence for a moment as I wondered how to respond. Behrouz's matter-of-fact attitude to the possibility of death left me speechless. He filled in the gap in conversation.

"There are, however, very many against Ahmadinejad – ordinary people who are angry that his obsession with nuclear power, along with the embargoes from the West, has drained our economy. The billions we get from oil are all spent on the military, new weapons research, and the continual search for atomic weapons. Ahmadinejad even has enemies amongst the Mullahs in Quom, our holiest city."

"Hard to believe," I said. "I thought the ruling Mullahs were all conservative disciples of the late Ayatollah Khomeini and now his successor Ayatollah Ali Khameini."

Behrouz gave me a sideways glance. "You know a lot – even pronounce the names correctly – but there is much for you to learn. Many clerics are opposed to religion being so deeply involved in politics. They see the hardliners as responsible for our worst problems: soaring food prices, the shaky economy, and our human rights record. Not all Iranians are villains; many long for a place in the open world rather than eternal condemnation from all the nations."

He eyed the landscape ahead of us for a while, then said, "I feel that we are somewhat like South Africa during the last years of Apartheid. All we lack is a Nelson Mandela. There are two who could possibly lead the way: one is the Grand Ayatollah Ali Hussein Motazeri, but he is old and his power weakens. Another is Hojjat al-Islam Mohsen Kadivar. Like Mandela, he was imprisoned. Since being freed he now works quietly with the reformists.

"I know of your mission. If you succeed, perhaps the floodgates of liberty will open, and the masses will see that all their sacrifices were in vain. Oil prices are at an all-time high, but the man in the street does not benefit. Our oil profits, besides going to the military and the two main nuclear plants, are also funneled to the mosques and the Mullahs who follow Khameini. I read in an underground pamphlet that Iran needs a government answerable not only to God but also to its own people."

Once more, I was amazed at the bravery of Behrouz and his comrades, and told him so.

"We do what we must," he replied laconically, and continued, "but in the same way, you and your friends are risking your lives in a very dangerous and difficult enterprise. We will do all we can to help, but remember that although your actions might shake the world, they are short-term solutions. We must think about the long term, and our help to you cannot jeopardise our long-term aims. If we have to make a choice, I want you to understand our thinking."

I was so impressed by Behrouz, and his calm logical thinking, that I wondered what he had done before joining the resistance. But I decided not to ask. Why dwell on what he had lost? He must have made peace with whatever he had left behind.

I changed the subject. "What, without giving away your cover, can you tell me about the Iranian opposition?"

"Little more than I have said," was the answer, but he did reveal a few more facts. There were bloggers assisting, and help from undercover US Special Forces units. Apparently, they came in at night, in black helicopters, and roamed the countryside on quad bikes with the objective of gathering intelligence. The Mojahedin-e-Khalk made contact with them from time to time, passing on information in exchange for much-needed supplies and hardware.

Thinking about the bloggers, I remembered a blog I had read by a Dr Zinn, which provided news about Iran and the opposition. When I mentioned it to Behrouz, he said it no longer existed. "Zinn has disappeared," he said. "No-one knows what happened to him."

Suddenly, I recognised the hill and thorn-brush behind which our hut was concealed.

"Back home," I said.

"Yes," he replied, "but there is no time to waste. We must head as soon as possible to Natanz and the mosque. My information is that our target is there now, and we must act quickly before he returns to Teheran. His public address takes place early tomorrow morning."

At the entrance to the hut, I climbed down from the half-track, and rejoined my comrades.

"The Haskins shoots well, but it is a brute to carry, and even with noise suppressors, makes an enormous noise when it's fired," I told them. "We will have time for one shot only; after that we must cut and run, lugging the Haskins with us. Have you got an exit strategy?" I asked Hassan. "If not, we can't risk it. Our primary mission is at the atomic site, and if we're caught before we get there everything has been in vain."

Hassan nodded. "You are right. One shot is all you will have, and we will be over half a kilometre away. But if the rifle is sighted in you should succeed.

And yes, we will have to get away fast. Alarms will be raised, and the town of Natanz blocked off. But on the positive side I do not expect the Iranians to connect the shooting with the atomic facility. They will most likely blame the local opposition."

Behrouz gave him a steely look. "Thanks," he said with a degree of irritation. "We will have to somehow alert our cell members to go undercover fast."

"I apologise," said Hassan. Turning to me, he continued, "I thought that with the noise suppressors, your shot would only be heard as a faint noise."

"Ask Behrouz," I responded, "the noise is still horrific. Remember that the rifle fires a .50 bullet, it is not a .25 handgun."

"Give us a little more time," Hassan said thoughtfully. "Behrouz and I must work together to re-draft our escape plan. You are right, Dieter, it must be entirely watertight to ensure you get to Natanz with no delay."

Hassan and Behrouz retreated into the hut, calling Gadir and Atash in a few minutes later, and emerged after some time with an elaborated plan.

Hassan filled me in. "Gadir, Behrouz and Atash will set off immediately to reconnoiter the surrounds of the mosque for a lying-up place as far away from the target as is safe within the rifle's range. Behrouz and will organise a decoy, a getaway vehicle and disguises to ease your escape from the scene, and Atash will finalise plans to help you sight the target. Gadir will call you with rendezvous coordinates near the lying-up site as soon as everything is in place. I will liaise with Behrouz regarding the details and brief you no later than dawn tomorrow."

Gadir, Behrouz and Farid were already donning their packs. Time was short, and I decided not to dwell on the uncertainties that remained. Instead, I would eat and grab a few hours sleep while I had the chance.

Chapter 34

The pain in my ear had subsided in the last 24 hours, but still I found myself lying awake. My mind churned over and over, trying to make sense of what Gadi and I had got ourselves into. What had seemed, at the outset, a very dangerous, but relatively straightforward mission, had now become complex – in fact, more than complex: foolhardy!

The more I thought, the more worried I became. Was the removal of the Iranian scientist really so vital that it was worth jeopardizing our mission to Natanz? I rearranged myself – for the fourth time in a matter of minutes – on the hard floor of the hut.

There was no guarantee we would get away with the assassination. But there would be no point in destroying the reactor site if it could be quickly rebuilt. Mossen had been the guiding force behind Iran's nuclear programme, and he would be almost impossible to replace. Despite being small fry compared to the destruction of an entire nuclear plant, his elimination might be the true death blow to Iran's nuclear aspirations.

I rolled over again, trying to get comfortable. But still the near future loomed large in my thoughts. In a few hours time, I would be carrying out a political assassination that might change the face of world history.

Suddenly, the cellphone in my hip pocket vibrated furiously. It was Gadi. *"Ha kol beseder gemoor,"* came his soft voice through the earpiece: "All OK."

I called softly to Hassan and the others. "We have a go!"

A minute later, the phone vibrated again, with a coded SMS message reading: 33°31'47" N—51°54'14"E. Our rendezvous point for the following day. I quickly keyed the coordinates into the cellphone and hand-held GPS systems, and deleted the message. One couldn't be too careful.

I spoke to Hassan: "Well, for better or worse, we have a position and the go-ahead."

Hassan immediately detailed the plan. "You must leave in the half-track just before dawn," he said. "Jalil will drive you; Farouk, Ibrahim and I will leave on foot. Our next rendezvous will be within the Natanz complex if you succeed in infiltrating the plant.

"You have one shot only. Make sure it counts," he reminded me. "Your signal that your quarry is mounting the podium will be a child's red, helium-filled balloon. Atash will be standing in the crowd with his sister's daughter, who will be carrying the balloon. When Mossen mounts the podium, Atash will wait for the area around him to be clear of other speakers and then release the balloon as if the child accidentally let it go. He will then send her on her way back to her home near Natanz.

"As soon as you see the balloon, take aim at the figure on the podium, fire, and get the hell out of your position. Jalil will guide you. Behrouz will bury the Haskins in a trench he and his comrades have dug nearby, while you and Gadir escape in the vehicle they have acquired for the purpose. We will part ways with Behrouz and his Mojahedin-e-Khalk comrades as soon as Mossen is disposed of – with suspicion falling on their members they will have their hands full. Jalil will accompany you to the uranium plant but will take his leave as soon as circumstances allow.

"During your practice shoot, Farouk and Ibrahim tied up some loose ends. Before we left the marshes, they had established contact with family friends who have been conscripted to work on the Natanz project. They were members of the Revolutionary Guards during the first Gulf war. They joined as a way of opposing Saddam Hussein after what he did to their territory. All the details have been resolved now; they are your ticket into the plant."

It seemed that the plan was far more organised than Gadi and I had first thought. "Why have you kept all this till the last minute?" I asked, bewildered.

"Very simple, Dieter. If you had been captured or run into trouble during your practice with the Haskins, it was better that you knew as little as possible. We cannot know whether you would withstand torture as an international spy and enemy of the country."

"I understand," I said, a little grudgingly. It seemed wrong that Gadi and I, the pivots of the whole mission, had been left out of the loop. Nor was it flattering that the possibility of my caving under torture had been an integral component of our compatriots' contingency planning.

Reassured by Hassan's elaboration of what lay ahead, I slept until about 05h00, when Jalil woke me.

"Time we left, Dieter," he said.

I sat up, yawned, stretched, and looked out of the doorway. The sun was not yet up, but there was a faint, rosy glow on the eastern horizon. The sky was growing lighter with every passing minute.

The last thing I did before we left was go outside for a long and satisfying pee. I had no idea when next I would have the opportunity. By the time I was done, Jalil had the motor of the half-track barely turning over. I lugged the heavy Haskins in to the back seat, and we set off.

For the first few minutes we traveled in silence. I knew next to nothing about Jalil, but my survival now depended on him. And vice versa.

"What made you join the Mojahedin-e-Khalk?" I asked.

"Behrouz joined from patriotism," he said. "For my part, it was partly revenge. My family were close to the late Shah. But what also drove me to join was the horrible corruption that had become commonplace among the Mullah elite."

This surprised me. "I always thought that they were a bunch of ascetics," I said.

"Far from it; just the opposite," he replied. "There are a few good men in the hierarchy, but they are either getting senile or being eliminated from the power structure."

His expression hardened. "There is a top man in the Iranian Parliamentary Investigations Committee – his name is Abbas Palizar. When I was a student, he gave a lecture at the university. It was unbelievable! He called the judiciary a cesspit of corruption, and was outspoken in naming the guilty parties.

"The regime have tried to discredit him, but he was very careful to keep thorough records. It took him over a year, but even though all his evidence is documented and video taped, no prosecutions have resulted.

"Fortunately, he is still trusted by the Supreme Leader of Iran, Ali Khameini. With his help, Khameini may eventually dislodge Ahmidenijad when his term of office ends in a few years' time.

Jalil lapsed into silence, concentrating on getting the vehicle over a patch of particularly rocky terrain. Then he continued – it was obviously a pet subject. "We are nearly there," he said, "but let me name some names. It will open your eyes to some of the corruption we have seen under the Mullahs.

"Ayatollah Emami-Kashani," he began, "got the license to operate the marble quarries in Dehbid, and now operates four state quarries for his own gain.

"Ayatollah Yazdi, and a group of his cohorts, got the Dena tyre company for a pittance, paid only 20 percent of the discounted price they agreed, and then floated it on the stock market. They walked away with a company worth over 600 million dollars.

"Then there is the story of Iran Khodo, which has the sole licence to make Peugeot cars in Iran. They were forced to give over 500 cars to members of the judiciary, and past heads of the Revolutionary Guards and the Intelligence Service."

As he talked, I traced our progress by GPS. We were nearly at our destination, and a tinny computerised voice from the system soon confirmed this.

We stopped the half track, and I dismounted, hauling out the Haskins. Gadi and Behrouz were nowhere to be seen, and I suppressed a sudden wave of panic – surely we could not have come so far only to have Gadi captured or killed and our mission betrayed.

The sun was now just below the horizon, and there were the faint signs of dawn daylight, although a few stars still shone above us. From a nearby tree, I heard the mournful cry of a nightjar. When I turned towards it, there was Gadi's mischievous face peering at us from the foliage.

"Hell, Gadi, you nearly scared the pants off me!" I exclaimed, alarmed at just how dulled my hearing had become since the blow to my ear. I reassured myself that it was Gadi's incredible stealth and not my damaged eardrum that was responsible for his sneaking up on us.

"Why not?" he smiled, "you have had a good night's sleep while the four of us had to foot-slog through the bush all night." While Behrouz and Atash had set out to locate a getaway vehicle, he and Farid had paced out the exact distance from the podium to a suitable knoll within firing range, one of them creating a diversion to distract the guards while the other did the fastest pacing they had ever dreamed of. Gadi reassured me that the pacing was accurate. They had an exact distance for my shot, but were a little the worse for wear.

"Sorry you got the raw end of the deal, Gadi, but hell, I have to shoot, and shoot well. I needed the rest," I retorted with a grin that belied the gravity of what we were about to undertake.

Behrouz interrupted, slinging the rifle onto his left shoulder. "We must get moving," he said, beckoning us forward. "Come! We must be in position before the sun is fully up."

He had chosen our rendezvous well; after a fairly short and cautious walk, we reached a small knoll. As we approached the edge of the rise, the mosque and town came into view. Behrouz handed over the Haskins.

"It's over to you now, Dieter," he said, his eyes meeting mine. As he spoke, the sun rose above the horizon. I lay down on the dew-damp grass, and set the bi-pod of the rifle firmly into the damp earth. Lying flat, with my legs spread-eagled behind me, I took the off the cover and looked through the optical sight.

It was a beautiful piece of engineering. There before me was the outline of what could only be the podium, set on a platform outside the mosque to accommodate a larger crowd than the temple would hold. I turned the sight to full focus, and the podium came into clear relief. I threw a few blades of grass into the air, to gauge the breeze, and the wind-speed. It was almost negligible, but I adjusted the sight very slightly to allow for wind drift.

Finally, I inserted one of the heavy rounds into the breech, and closed it shut with a slight click.

Looking to my rear, I saw the other three lying concealed in the sparse brush. Thanks to the knoll, it was unlikely our retreating bodies would be seen from the town once my job here was done, even if the shot rang out as loudly as I expected.

In the meantime, there was nothing more I could do until our target arrived. The grass auditorium would fill up long before his arrival, and we had to hope that no-one took a leisurely walk in our direction. Once the day got hotter, that seemed unlikely.

Using the distance Gadir had paced out the night before, I took my time distance-adjusting the sight. With nothing better to do, I then checked the entire set-up once more, for safety's sake. It was all spot on.

I lay my head on my hands, warning the others to wake me if I drifted off. My body relaxed, but my mind churned on. I thought of Adinah, and that wonderful day at the beach in Netanya. I remembered how Shimon had looked during those last 24 hours in hospital, and silently thanked him for the great sacrifice he had made in saving Gadi and I. Finally, my thoughts moved on to our mission, what we had endured, and what still lay ahead of us.

I rolled over and looked up at the bright blue sky. The sun had risen, and high above me I saw a kite circling on the wind currents from the earth below. Far to the west, vultures were also wheeling around, attracted to the dead or dying body of some unfortunate animal. All nature seemed oblivious to the horrors this day would entail and the grave threat to all existence that lay beneath the soil of Natanz.

It was hard to believe that pear orchards had once covered the site of the nuclear plant – "The best and tastiest pears in all Iran," according to Behrouz. He had also told me that the grave of Darius III, once king of Persia, lay not far from the town. Nearby was the grave of Bessus, the Persian *satrap** who had killed Darius because he was about to surrender to Alexander the Great, and was in turned killed by Alexander.

During my post army University days, I had joined the university dramatic society, and played Bessus in Terrence Rattigan's "Adventure Story." All these fragments of memory and history seemed strangely poignant on the cusp of what I was about to do.

* *Persian: Provincial governor.*

I felt a tap on my arm. Gadir had crept forward to indicate the amphitheatre, which was filling up rapidly. My heart began to beat harder as the appointed time approached. I took up my sniping position, legs flat on the ground in an inverted V, my elbows on the grass and the stock of the Haskins firm against my right shoulder. I looked intently through the optical scope as a robed figure mounted the platform, wondering if this was my man. Any minute now!

And there it was: a red balloon, rising into the sky. I heard Behrouz retreating on his stomach; perhaps the last I would ever hear of him. He was to plant a grenade in the petrol tank of the half-track, its locking pin replaced with a rubber band that would dissolve quickly in the fuel, causing an explosion that would throw pursuers off our tracks in about 10 minutes' time.

I focused on the head of the man at the microphone, delaying for a few moments to give Atash and his niece enough time to leave the scene. I watched the rhythm of the man's movements for two or three minutes. From this distance he seemed to have a distinct rhetorical style, and was given to dramatic pauses. This gave me a sense of the predictability of his position from one moment to the next.

I placed my finger through the trigger guard, softly gripped the trigger, and waited for his next pause, willing myself to follow through. This would be my first live mark, and it was nothing like aiming for a lifeless cardboard cut-out. When the moment came, I knew I had no choice. I very gently pulled the trigger.

There came a roar of sound, and through the sight I saw the man collapse on the stage. For a few seconds I was frozen in shock, and almost immediately Behrouz grabbed the gun from my hands. Jalil hauled me up by the arm, and we quickly headed away from the scene.

Minutes later, as we moved closer and closer toward our rendezvous at the getaway vehicle, I heard an enormous blast as our decoy kicked in. A pillar of smoke rose into the sky behind us, frightening way the once soaring kites.

Chapter 35

The sounds of distant shouts and barked orders carried on the air as Gadir and I hurried after the others.

"Faster, faster," hissed Gadir. "We are nearly there, but we must hurry. We still have to change our clothing when we get to the Jeep."

A few moments later, we were there. The camouflaged Jeep was an old American model, most likely inherited from the days when the US had been a close ally of the late Shah of Iran. Iranian military uniforms lay in plastic bags on the floor of the vehicle. Gadir and I transformed into non-commissioned officers in record time and, with Jalil at the wheel in the garb of a major, left the mosque precinct, heading due north on a winding trail.

The Natanz nuclear complex soon came into sight. It was nothing like I had imagined it to be from the photographs we had been shown during briefings in Tzal'aim. There they had shown us a satellite photograph indicating the outlines, tunnel entrance and work in progress. This was the real thing: square two-storey buildings, coated in glossy white paint and festooned with Iranian flags. From the outside, it looked more like a modern government public complex, than a uranium enrichment facility.

"Sit up straight," hissed Jalil, "and look as if you belonged here. Our arrival is unscheduled, and will cause a little chaos, but I have passes for the three of us. Just sit quietly and look bored."

I tried to comply, but it was easier said than done. Here Gadi and I were: two Israelis about to enter the most heavily guarded place in Iran. My heart was pounding, and try as I might, I couldn't stop the sweat from leaking out of every pore in my body.

A red-and-white striped boom halted our progress, and a full squad of guards, armed with heavy-calibre automatic rifles, stepped up to meet us. "Passes! Passes!" barked the officer in charge. Casually, Jalil handed over our passes, and it suddenly dawned on me why Ali had photographed us back at the marshes. It seemed there had been a great deal of behind-the-scenes work to get our mission moving forward.

The officer in charge of the guard post looked at our passes very thoroughly and motioned us out of the Jeep. A second officer patted each of us down as the leading officer paced past us, examining our features minutely and comparing them to the passes.

My uniform was now drenched with sweat, and as he grasped my shoulder and motioned me to look up at him, I thanked God for the burning hot sunlight pouring down on us. Trying desperately not to show my fear, I looked him straight in the eyes.

To my surprise, he looked across at Atash, a defiant look on his face. "I have a bad feeling about this one," he said, indicating me with a jerk of his chin. "Strip search him!" Unsure whether my Farsi would pass as fluent, I held my peace. Jalil gave a firm nod, yielding to the guard's authority despite the higher rank his uniform communicated.

With my compatriots standing stiffly alongside, I was forced to discard my clothing, and stood sweating in my underwear, while a squaddie went through my discarded clothing, feeling every stitch in the fabric. I counted my single blessing: that our armaments and electronic equipment were all in the hands of Hassan and Behrouz. With the help of Ibrahim and Farouk, they were to smuggle what we needed into the plant once we had infiltrated the site.

After my clothes were returned to me, the officer turned back to Atash. "What is your purpose here?" he demanded. "Your men were not expected on this base."

"Officer," said Jalil, "I respect your position: I have not questioned your authority even though I outrank you. Here are our orders and travel passes. My men and I are skilled radar operators, and were instructed to make our way here with all speed. As you know, there have been rumours among the international community of an impending strike against our nuclear assets. We were sent to reinforce your defensive capabilities in case such an attack materialises. It would seem to me that there has been the usual communication breakdown." He shook his head empathically, adding, "It makes me very impatient when headquarters do not have the respect to inform our officers on the ground."

"Indeed. I should have been informed," the officer grunted. He did not apologise for the treatment he had meted out, but he had clearly been softened by the rapport Jalil had so cleverly constructed. "Your documents appear to be in order," he said. "Omeed! Go with them to the empty barracks; there are spare beds there. Let them wait there while I contact the radar unit."

The guard ushered us back into the jeep, and, sitting upfront with Jalil, directed him to a group of long white-painted buildings. It was almost identical to the barracks in the camp at Tzal'aim in the Negev.

I was still worried sick by the reception we had endured, not to mention the possibility that contact with the radar unit might give us away as imposters to the chief guard. I exchanged a tense look with Gadi, but catching Jalil's eye, it seemed he had no worries at all. He grinned when he saw my anxious face.

"Not to worry, Dieter, that scene at the barrier was all put up," he said. "The officer's name is Arash, and he is one of the Madan. He has been paid a year's salary in gold coins, with the promise of the same again, if we succeed. He didn't need much encouragement; his sister was violently raped by the camp commandant three months ago, and he could not take direct revenge. Behrouz knew what had happened, though, and gave him this opportunity to regain his honour. Omeed, too, has been rewarded in advance, and will keep watch for us and inform us if anything goes wrong. We have arranged everything, including the equipment you will need and your route into the tunnel. We have been working on this plan since you were first briefed in Israel."

An expression of shock enveloped my face, and he smiled. "Yes, we have known about you for some time, 'Dieter'," he said meaningfully.

I was still flummoxed. "But... why us? It seems to me your own people could have done the job just as well without the two of us."

"Perhaps," Jalil reflected, "But it is your country that faces annihilation by the uranium enriched here, and your aircraft that will be doing the job. Under the circumstances no nation would entrust such a mission to citizens of another country. Your top people wanted their own men at the hard edge, but it is a pleasure to help you succeed."

I sat on a bunk, absorbing the new information. Gadir began: "So, our equipment...," but Jalil silenced him with the answer. "Behrouz and Hassan have it all in hand," he said. "The moment the guard officer was bribed and on side, we selected this barracks. Farouk and Ibrahim, together with a big team of former marsh Arabs, have been hard at work for three months, digging a tunnel, with a carefully concealed entrance about 500 metres from the camp perimeter.

"The tunnel has been carefully re-enforced with thick wooden boards and the ceiling propped up with poles cut from eucalyptus trees – strong and pliable. They have even managed to rig up an electric line and string electric light bulbs through its entire length."

I was stunned. This was truly incredible. But then again, tunnels were a staple of underground activity. Closer to our own part of the world, Hamas was forever digging under the Rafah border to smuggle arms through Egypt into Gaza.

The more I heard from Hassan and his Iranian rebel team, the more impressed I became. This was no Karameh after all! Obviously the Mossad in Israel had done some serious forward planning and put together a well organised and cohesive plan. Gadir and I were only two small but vital cogs in a well assembled and well oiled gear-box. And, like everyone else, we had been subject to the organisation's notorious need-to-know policy.

I looked over at Gadi, and he winked at me, raising his usual eyebrow. "I am sure that they had a Plan B, and failing that, a Plan C," he smiled. "It seems we are minnows swimming in a vast dam, but somehow avoiding the fisherman's nets," he continued. We slipped back into silence, and my mind wandered beyond the armoured perimeter of the plant and back to the Kibbutz Ma'ayan Tsvi, where I had fished with friends in days gone by.

A faint knocking from the corner of the room stirred me from my reverie with a shock. My hand snatched my side, but found no weapon. We were defenceless! But suddenly, with a start of relief, I realised the sound must be our team arriving from the tunnel.

Jalil moved to a bundle of prayer mats under the last bunk in the corner of the room, filling us in as he went. "We have to move fast. The tunnel serves two purposes: first, it is our entry and exit route, and second, your equipment will be stored in a hollowed out chamber at the entrance, just under here." He stamped his foot on the trap door, and received a dot-dot-dot-dash from the other side – the V signal.

Chapter 36

Hassan was the first to emerge, in his usual snow-white robes. How the hell did he keep so clean, I wondered. After the last 36 hours, I had never felt so dirty in all my life.

After him came Ibrahim and his older brother. The cast in Farouk's eye looked even more ominous than usual, and once again I suppressed the disquieting feeling that he might not be quite what he seemed.

The once empty barracks now seemed full to overflowing. Heaven forbid the Iranians should decide to do a surprise kit inspection – they would catch our whole team in one fell swoop. Fortunately, Omeed was on the front line, standing guard outside.

Hassan immediately took the lead; he seemed to have a penchant for the commanding role.

"Everything has proceeded smoothly up to now," he said, "but, as the English say, 'there's many a slip twixt the cup and the lip.' We are very near to the end game, and having made it this far we cannot afford to fail.

"Dieter, Gadir, the GPS beacons are in a hollow under the trapdoor, along with plastic Glock pistols that should evade electronic surveillance. There are seven fully stocked kit bags, containing maps, hand-held GPS sets and compasses, a well as emergency rations, bottled water and first aid kits. There is also a British mini-mini machine pistol. In addition, you will find an assortment of hand grenades, claymore mines, and one disassembled RPG.* Of course, we hope not to need any of this

---

* *Rocket-propelled grenade.*

gear. We will invest our best efforts in keeping our work discreet and getting out of here with little or no disturbance to the usual running of things.

"My information from SIS is that the attack is imminent. We have only days left to get it all together." SIS must have obtained this information from the Mossad, but Hassan was obviously taking care to preserve our covers even at this late hour.

Farouk stepped forward. "What about the final payment for all our work?" he asked, and received a scathing look from Gadir.

"The dinars owed to you are in Ali's possession," Hassan reaffirmed. "You will receive them from him on your return to the marshes if we succeed. For the second installments to Omeed and the head guard Arash, gold coins are in a safe place, known to Atash and Behrouz. The coins will be handed over to them at an agreed rendezvous location by an agent of Mojahedin-e-Khalk within 24 hours of successful completion of our mission."

Gadir interrupted, clearly impatient with this talk of payment. "After the beacons have been planted and activated, we will exit the plant via the tunnel and go our separate ways on the other side. Let there be no more talk of compensation; each man has been briefed and there will be no time for further negotiations during our escape."

Hassanbrought the ill will to a diplomatic close by issuing further instructions. "Jalil, it is time for us to part company. Take the Jeep and leave the plant on the pretext of being recalled to assist in investigating this morning's assassination. We thank you and wish you all the best as you continue to fight your enemies. The Mullahs will not collapse overnight and the attack on Natanz will enrage them beyond endurance."

He went on: "Farouk, Ibrahim, as you know, the most important part of your task lies ahead." Turning to Gadi and I, he explained, "Two of the brothers' friends work underground here, clearing out the rubble from new tunnels being excavated. We have warned them to go awol to avoid the disaster that may befall the plant, so there will be two openings that you can fill.

"Gadir, we are relying on you to lead this part of the operation, you speak natural Arabic, and can easily pass as one from the marshes. There are bound to be questions from your workmates as to why you have replaced Farouk's friends."

To Farouk, Hassan went on, "You must now leave this place and return via the gate. Once you have signed in and returned to the workforce, you will tell the foreman that your friends have lung and chest infections from their long time working underground, and that you have requested transfers from the maintenance unit to help your team out. Omeed will bring Gadir and Dieter in as the replacements a little later on."

As Farouk disappeared through the trapdoor, Hassan looked first at Gadi, and then at me with his piercing gaze. "The two of you will need at least two days to get to know your new jobs. This will not arouse suspicion; after all, you are two rookies from maintenance. You can use the opportunity to seek out a place to plant the GPS beacons. And don't make it too difficult to reach and activate them when we receive Code Red."

It was strange to say the least that Gadi and I were getting our final briefing from an Arabian Sheik who was also a British SIS agent. But by this point in the mission I had surrendered to the unexpected. Looking around at our motley band of men, each with different backgrounds and agendas, I was reminded of *The A Team*, an American TV programme I loved as a boy. The cigar-puffing commanding officer always said the same thing as a mission came into its own: "I love it when a plan comes together." Right now, I felt the same way.

"Come," said Hassan, "I have new outfits for you two." He descended into the cavern under the barracks, and returned with bundles of old clothing after a little scuffling. Gadi and I began to put them on. "We're doing more changes than the girls at the Surf Crest Hotel," I whispered to Gadi, who grinned back at me.

Soon, we were standing in worn overalls, with large plastic ID cards slung around our necks. Our heads capped with safety helmets, we certainly looked like building workers, and our special-issue boots blended in perfectly, dirty and dust-caked as they were.

"Follow Omeed," said Hassan, "it's nearly 09h30, and your new shift will be assembling. Ibrahim and I will see you again only after you have planted the beacons"

At the main barrack square, a bunch of rough, tough workers were indeed assembling. Farouk had obviously worked with this lot before, as they all seemed to know him. His explanations seemed to have satisfied them.

The work was hard. New tunnels were being excavated, branching off from the main tunnel entrance to the underground works. Obviously, the Natanz operation was being enlarged at a furious pace. After a day stooped in the passages, shoveling and loading little carts with rubble, Gadi and I collapsed onto our bunks, almost too tired to speak.

"This is certainly hard labour," Gadi sighed after a few minutes. "Did you see any likely spots for the beacons?"

"Not really," I replied, "but I'll make damn sure I do tomorrow. This is no job for me; I'd rather be shot at. Tomorrow we'll just be two more guys in the regular team, so there will be fewer eyes on us. We can hide the GPS beacons in our lunch pails so we can take the first opportunity to plant them."

With that, we headed to the ablution block. The day's rigours had left us stinking with sweat, but we hadn't been particularly clean when we arrived at the plant. I was looking forward to my first shower in several days, and, after that, some food in the mess hall where we would join Farouk. Army food was bad at the best of times, but it would be better than the ready-to-eat rations we had been forcing down up to now.

The next day, we assembled again under a blazingly hot sun. We drew our lunch rations of pita bread, humus, and yogurt, and tucked the food into lunch pails in which the plastic-wrapped beacons were already concealed.

As we went underground, we began surreptitiously scouting for hiding places. But we didn't have to look far. A maintenance team was moving oil lamps from the mouth of the tunnel down to the point a little deeper where the passages branched out. Left behind were the empty cavities where the lamps had been drilled into the entrance walls.

The shift could not end soon enough for me. I was both mentally and physically exhausted. On our return trip up the tunnel, I paused, as if to catch my breath, leaned against the rock wall as if for support, and inserted the small beacon deep into one of the cavities. Gadi, who was walking with a separate group behind me, followed my example on the opposite wall. He had already prepared a handful of dirt to thrust in behind his beacon.

Back at the hut, we reported back using our secure cellphones before collapsing, exhausted, onto our bunks once again. Usually, anxiety about the impending coded call would have kept me awake for hours, but after some watery mutton and carrot stew at the mess hall, I crumpled with fatigue and fell into a deep sleep almost as soon as I closed my eyes.

I had hardly woken up the next morning when I felt my cellphone vibrating furiously under my thin pillow. I put it to my ear and heard what I had been waiting for. "Code Red! Code Red!"

Switching to SMS mode, I tapped in the acknowledgement. Looking over at Gadi, I gave him a meaningful nod. We looked long and hard at each other. At least 100 aircraft were now en route to Iran.

A moment later, we heard a knocking at the trap door. The V signal: dot-dot-dot-dash. I ran to raise the door, and Hassan appeared through the opening.

"We received the message," I confirmed.

"And I have received exit coordinates for the rendezvous with the sub," Hassan replied. The three of us locked eyes in grave silence. None of us voiced what we all realised: to activate the beacons, Gadi and I would have to complete another eight hour shift underground. The flying time from Israel to Iran was much less than that, meaning the two of us would still be underground when the strike came.

Hassan's piercing stare seemed to read my mind. "We will find a way to get you out," he said solemnly. Gadi and I looked at each other with grim, set faces. This was our mission, regardless of whether we became victims of friendly fire.

After the morning assembly, we walked leaden footed to the tunnel entrance. Once there, I squared my shoulders, braced myself, and stumbled dramatically as we approached the beacons' hiding place. Grasping the wall for support, I grimaced and rubbed my ankle. Gadir hurried to my side as the rest of the workforce trudged on.

"Not to worry, he has only twisted his ankle," Gadi reassured a passerby. "Go ahead, I will help him to get back to work."

As soon as attention had dwindled, I reached into the cavity and activated the GPS. We then rushed to other side and did the same there. For better or worse, our task was done, and in the nick of time. Our works foreman, Akhtar, was rushing back towards the entrance from the belly of the excavations.

"No shamming here!" he barked, "we are short staffed, and behind schedule. You pain is not my problem. Get on with the job!"

Gone was any hope of absconding back to the barracks while the coast was clear. Gadi and I trudged into the deepening darkness, with me limping theatrically. I was counting the minutes that had elapsed since I had heard the code word. Another three hours and all hell would break loose at Natanz, with Gadi and I trapped at the epicentre of the explosion.

As we set to work, bent double with our spades, I tried to concentrate on the work at hand. But grueling as it was, the physical labour was mentally tedious. My mind pored over the fate Gadi and I were about to endure. I knew it would be a case of *"pro patria mori,"* but that was cold comfort. There would be no military funeral for an undercover mission like ours, nothing to tell Adinah why I had disappeared. In death, I would be a disappointment in love once again. I cursed the army for snatching away another chance at happiness

As for poor Gadi, his situation was far worse. He had a wife and family, whom he had left with very little notice. They would never know what had happened to him, and there would be no recompense from any government source. At least I was single. I didn't regret the alimony that my ex-wives would no longer receive.

I filled the compact railway trucks with sand and stone, unable to comprehend how, after the long and tortuous journey that had brought us here, and all the dangers we had somehow surmounted, we could now die in an unknown and unmarked grave.

The barking of orders broke into my thoughts. I looked up to see Arash speaking harshly to the works foreman.

"What the hell are these two men doing here?" he demanded of Akhtar. "They are skilled radar operators, not common workmen."

Akhtar bumbled a bewildered response. "I only know that they were drafted to fill in for the men who were short on my team. Farouk, one of my team leaders, requested them. Sir, as you know, we have been commanded to finish this work by month end, and we are already behind schedule."

"To hell with you and your targets!" Arash responded, grabbing Gadi and I by the shoulders, "the rest of the team can work longer and harder. Have you not heard that foreign dogs might be planning an attack here? And where is this Farouk?"

The argument did not last much longer. Akhtar was glad to push Farouk forward as the straw man for the debacle, and I breathed a sigh of relief as Arash hustled the three of us away. Hassan had come through for us as promised. In a low voice, I asked whether Arash and Omeed would be leaving with us. Eyes front, he muttered that he would find his co-worker and follow us as soon as they had an opportunity.

Back at the barracks, Hassan and Ibrahim were waiting for us. "No time to waste," Hassan urged, making his way toward the trap door. "Grab your kitbags and follow us."

We nodded dumbly, and followed his orders, grabbing our bags in the entrance hollow before heading down the long, winding tunnel. It was dimly lit by weak electric bulbs and damp from the water seeping through the earthen roof. Progress was slow, since we had to tread carefully. An inadvertent slip and an injury now could prevent us from escaping the area in time to avoid the impending air strike.

At last, we reached the escape-tunnel exit, concealed by a plug of brush that we moved aside, and replaced once we emerged into the sunlight. Unexpectedly, Farouk turned back toward me, and I caught my breath at the sudden movement. But his hard face and sinister eye were oriented toward the entrance we had just closed up, and, turning around, I saw that Gadi, too, had picked up a sound.

"Someone is coming," he hissed. But it was too late to move. The brush moved aside, and to our relief it was Omeed who emerged from the dark mouth. He strode toward me, stretching out his hand in what I took to be a gesture of mutual congratulation. But, as I reached out to grasp the hand he offered, I saw that in fact it held a deadly Glock pistol.

Chapter 37

"You are not leaving until I receive my second payment," Omeed declared, raising the gun. "Where is the gold?"

Hassan intervened, "You know very well it is being held in trust for you by the Mojahedin-e-Khalk. Where is Arash? We made the same agreement with both of you."

"Arash is a fool. He will not be interrupting us; I locked the door of the barracks and once I receive my payment I will consider whether or not to have mercy and let him through."

"There is no time for that!" Farouk protested, his face drawn with shock at what had befallen a fellow son of the Madan. "He was assured safe passage out if we succeeded. We must return!" he cried, looking to Hassan for confirmation.

But there was no going back. Omeed and the Glock pistol were blocking our path. "Either I get my money now, or this one dies first," he said, bringing the gun to my ear.

"Peace, Omeed," I said through clenched teeth, "I have some gold coins with me, for an emergency. Wait, and I will give them to you."

"Where are they?" he shouted, as my three cohorts looked around nervously, afraid that his raised voice would draw attention. "Let me see for myself!"

"They are concealed in my boots," I replied quietly. "Allow me to take them out and I will hand them over to you." Omeed stood back slightly, the gun slightly lowered but still pointed in my direction.

"Take your boots off, very slowly," he instructed. "Very carefully and very slowly." I did as he asked, and he snatched up the boots as soon as I freed my feet.

"I see no gold here, you lying dog!" he yelled, dropping the boots and jerking the pistol back to my head.

I raised my hands in surrender. "There is a secret compartment," I said, slowly. "I will get them for you." Moving incredibly slowly, I pulled the boots back from where he had slung them on the ground.

"This is where the gold is hidden," I said clearly, slowly fingering the heel of the boot. I pressed the raised dot and slowly guided the heel out. The Kruger Rands shone brightly in the sunlight.

"Not enough!" he barked as I emptied the coins into his hand, "I am owed a year's salary. What about your little friend? Has he also got some gold hidden away?"

Gadi shrank away. "I cannot spare it all, Omeed," he said, "but I can give you some." He began untying his laces.

"Give it to me now; all of it!" Omeed hissed, "or I will shoot your generous friend over here."

Hassan, Farouk and Ibrahim stood by, helpless to intervene, as Omeed held the Glock inches from my head. Their faces were frozen with tension.

"Here," said Gadi meekly, as he slowly rose from the floor, holding a boot before him as if in offering to Omeed. But all of a sudden, he seemed to move into fast forward.

"This is what you have earned!" Gadi cried. As the heel swung out, he lunged toward Omeed like a striking snake, clutching the *sakin yapani* that was hidden there.

As he slashed at Omeed's throat, a slit opened like a second mouth in the skin. A bloody avalanche spurted out, and Gadir pushed Omeed's twitching body to the ground.

Farouk fell to his knees at Omeed's side, riffling through his pockets.

"Farouk! There is no time to lose! We must bury the body out of sight immediately," Hassan whispered. But Farouk had found what he was looking for: the key to the barracks door. Seeing this, Hassan gave a nod of affirmation as Farouk made his way back into the tunnel. I looked after him, impressed by a man who would head back into a ticking time bomb to save an acquaintance. He was a better man than me, I thought. What an irony that an accident of birth had made him appear the opposite.

"Let's get to work," said Hassan, taking hold of Omeed's lifeless body. "We must hide his body at once and get to the coast as soon as possible to rendezvous with the exit submarine."

As fast as possible, counting the minutes, we buried Omeed under a collection of rocks and soil. When the grim work was done, we set off at a jog towards our escape rendezvous, guided by cloth maps and the ever-ready GPS in Hassan's hand. Ibrahim remained behind, awaiting his brother's return. Silently, we wished Farouk and Arash good fortune in escaping the nuclear complex before the strike took place.

The submarine would wait no longer than was safe under the circumstances, and there were still several kilometres to go. Keeping up the pace, I thanked God for the training we had endured back home. After just over two hours of careful deviations around small villages and itinerant herdsmen, with the sky darkening with storm clouds overhead, we caught sight of the blue waters of the Persian Gulf just ahead of us, and a rubber dinghy moored at the shore.

An instant later, we picked up a hum in the distance, and with incredible speed it swelled into a wall of thunderous sound as squadrons of low-flying Israeli F15's and F16's swooped over us, greeted by bursts of anti-aircraft fire. One of our planes burst into flames, and I prayed that that the pilot had ejected in time. Our mission was almost over, but theirs had only just begun.

We were only metres away from the floating vessel when the world seemed to explode in a blaze of fire and smoke. The plant at Natanz was no more, and I hoped desperately that our accomplices had got away in time.

At the helm of the dinghy was someone I recognised: Motti Ben Shahar, an old friend from Netanya, who was now an officer in the Elite Shayettet naval force, modeled on the American Navy Seals.

"*Shalom*, Dani, welcome back," he said, and I felt an enormous relief at hearing my real name and reassuming my old identity. "*Mazeltov** to you and your friends on a job well done."

The sub was just half a kilometre offshore, and the Iranian military was far too busy warding off the air strike to notice four men floating off to sea as the country burned.

* *Hebrew: Congratulations.*

"By the way, Dani, that was quite a fireworks display you and your friends gave us!" Motti smiled, "better even than what our Mayor Miriam gives us on Independence day!"

"Yes," I said thoughtfully, looking out at the storm of destruction we were leaving behind. "You're right. This is our very own Independence Day – independence at long last from the Iranian threat."

And so we moved away from Iran, the land of my mother's birth. We were leaving good men behind to their fates, and taking with us secrets that could never be shared. But here we were. Alive, and on our way back, finally, to our own homeland – a now much safer Israel.

www.ingramcontent.com/pod-product-compliance
Ingram Content Group UK Ltd.
Pitfield, Milton Keynes, MK11 3LW, UK
UKHW041437180426
11947UKWH00007B/500